PRAISE FOR

LUST BITES ANTHOLOGY
VOLUME ONE

Amuse Me ~ Everything about this story made me swoon and really believe that there is the perfect person out there for all of us. Kudos to Lexie Davis for making me a believer! ~ *Romance Junkies*

Faithful Beginnings is a fantastic start to a new series that I hope goes far for Ms. Thorn. ~ *Joyfully Reviewed*

Lust Detector can be described in three words, short, sweet, and hot! There is nothing lacking in this very short read. Despite its length it will have you reaching for the nearest fan or man and if neither is available a cold shower. If you like your erotica hot, don't miss this one! ~ *Simply Romance Reviews*

Hot and Humid ~ I definitely did not want the story to end, and would recommend this story to anyone interested in spending time reading purely for enjoyment. ~ *Simply Romance Reviews*

Misery Loves Company ~ Ellen Ashe is a master at making the pulses jump and the thoughts whirl with her stories. Misery Loves Company is another brilliant example of that talent.
~ *Kwips & Critiques*

Confessions of a Nympho ~ Ace and Tatiana's encounters were in a word - explosive. Confessions of a Nympho was a dynamite story of opposites attracting and you should check it out today. ~ *Simply Romance Reviews*

LUST BITES
ANTHOLOGY
VOLUME ONE

AMUSE ME
LEXIE DAVIS

FAITHFUL BEGINNINGS
LACEY THORN

LUST DETECTOR
ANN CORY

HOT AND HUMID
SHERMAINE WILLIAMS

MISERY LOVES COMPANY
ELLEN ASHE

CONFESSIONS OF A NYMPHO
ASHLEY LADD

LUST BITES ANTHOLOGY - Volume One
ISBN # 978-1-906590-31-4
Amuse Me ©Copyright Lexie Davis 2008
Faithful Beginnings ©Copyright Lacey Thorn 2008
Lust Detector ©Copyright Ann Cory 2008
Hot and Humid ©Copyright Shermaine Williams 2008
Misery Loves Company ©Copyright Ellen Ashe 2008
Confessions of a Nympho ©Copyright Ashley Ladd 2008
Cover Art by Anne Cain ©Copyright 2008
Interior text design by Claire Siemaszkiewicz
Total-E-Bound Publishing

Published in 2008 by Total-E-Bound Publishing 1 Faldingworth Road, Spridlington, Market Rasen, Lincolnshire, LN8 2DE, UK.

Total-E-Bound Publishing is an imprint of Total-E-Ntwined Limited.

Manufactured in the USA.

AMUSE ME

Lexie Davis

Dedication

To my grandfather.
Words cannot describe how much you mean to me.

Chapter One

Wilmington, North Carolina

I sat at my computer stuck in a writing rut and listening to the Eagles on my iPod. My boyfriend had left me at the same time I was due to turn in my latest erotic romance to my editor — and I had nothing.

I massaged my temples hoping something would strike a chord in my brain. A mere spark of an idea that would be fun to write, fun to read and leaving my fans breathless and begging for more. The more I thought about it, the harder it was to convert my thoughts to the blank computer screen.

The blinking curser mocked me as I stared at the white page. Dammit, Rich may have fucked my life up but he wasn't going to take a way my passion for writing. I wouldn't let him, no matter what it cost.

In high school, young love blooms like tulips in the spring — sometimes developing into loving, lasting relationships and sometimes setting one up for heartache. Rich, I thought, would be the loving lasting relationship kind of guy but, boy, was I wrong. We'd dated throughout high school and college. I'd heard sex changed the relationship, but I was stupid and naive. Rich was a sexual being and aroused feelings within me no other man had. If only those feelings had been mutual.

I'm twenty-five years old and it took me seven years to discover the man I'd thought I loved—the mushy, gushy kind of love—had cheated on me. Not once or twice—no that was too easy. He'd fucked every girl he'd come in contact with.

For six months he'd been out of my life, yet he still haunted my dreams. I'd found out two days ago, from my best friend, that his latest conquest was having his baby. The more I thought about it, the more I hated him. I wanted payback. I needed it for some weird reason.

I started typing, letting my anger fuel the words on paper, my fingers flying across the keyboard as my thoughts sputtered from my brain. For once in my life, I was taking all the writing advice I'd thought was crap and putting it to good use. I wrote what I knew.

I made my real life story an act of fiction.

A few hours later I'd plotted, planned and brainstormed about all the events I'd experienced and a few from my imagination as well. I had a five-page plan of events, a storyline and the perfect ending. Funny, how something so obvious was hidden right under my nose.

My side of the story mixed with a little imagination would be my vengeance. After all, paybacks always were hell…

* * * *

Atlanta, Georgia — Erotic Romance Convention

"Montana Raine, I just love your work!" A fan approached me at my designated table where I was signing of my newest release, *Against All Odds*. "Would you please sign my book?"

I signed fans' copies until my hand felt like it was going to fall off. Writer's cramp settled deep into my bones, aching as the line slowly shortened. My friends, fellow writers, and I used to joke about the kind of people show up at things like these. At the first signing I attended, we'd had to call security because a man had read my friend Jenny's novel and stolen a pair of crotchless panties like those she'd described in her book from a nearby lingerie store. Thankfully, that was the only illegal action we'd ever encountered. Most of the time it was only creepy stares from passing men, judging us by the things we write. An overwhelming number of fans desperately want to know if I've "researched" everything I write. Though I'm an erotic romance novelist, even I consider some things to be a bit private. But on the other hand there is a disclosure saying, "this book is a work of the author's imagination." Some things are just…fantasy.

Except for my newest book. Whoever said real life doesn't make interesting fiction is a fool. *Against All Odds* was a bestseller, topping two of the most proclaimed lists in the country. The book was available in just about every medium known to man where anyone could read it. Lucky for me people actually *wanted* to. I did however spice things up a bit and focus more on my cheating boyfriend being the jackass he is, but there were more real aspects in it from my life than would normally show up in my novels. Rich's inspiration was nonetheless villain perfect, bringing me to a key point of my story.

Not that the heroine and the villain had anything going on. No, she had the old cliché every woman loves. Tall, dark and handsome—with a nice car, great job and for once, a brain. The hero was her own personal sex slave.

"Megan." My editor Kaitlin Moore sashayed over to my table, breaking the line to talk to me. "Can you find time to take a break? The new CEO of Quicksand Books wants to talk to you about a book deal. He's waiting in the backroom as we speak."

Quicksand Books, Inc. had recently made a few business changes, and if they were still going to keep me on board as one of their authors, then so be it. I'd make the time to meet with them. They'd stuck by me throughout my career, me being one of their very first clients. We were sort of old friends.

"Of course."

After finishing out my autograph line, I took a few seconds to get a bottle of water from a Coke machine and went searching for my editor. At thirty, Kaitlin was a few years older than me but knew more about this business than I possibly could after only three years of writing and selling my work to her company. Michele Lockland-Stewart had started the company with her own money. Now she was on maternity leave, and from what I had heard, the new owner, her brother Blake, was quite a drill sergeant.

"Kaitlin," I said, coming up to my editor at her table. The conference held at the Atlanta convention centre had aspiring authors from all around the country pitching their current works-in-progress, begging and pleading for any and all editor's and agent's attention. It had taken three minutes for me to make my way through the crowd to her table.

"Oh, Megan." She stood and turned to her assistant. "Debbie, please man the crowd for a second. I'll be right back."

She led me through the large room, past several editors I knew and writers who were my close friends. The faint smell of roses filled my nose before I realised a big name writer had received two-dozen roses from an adoring fan. *Must suck to be her.*

We made it to the other side of the room, bypassing table after table until we finally entered a narrow hallway off-limits to the general public. In a way, being taken to the back to meet a guy seemed a bit creepy—even for me.

"Sorry about pulling you away from your fans. Mr. Lockland wanted to see you right away. He's a bit shy. That's why he's hanging out in the staff lounge." She stepped aside opening a door for me.

The room we entered was a typical lounge. A black couch sat in the middle of the room with a TV pointing directly at it. Round restaurant-style tables with matching white chairs crammed the small kitchenette—perfect for slacking on the job. On the couch, however, sat a man with his back to us watching a football game on the TV. I couldn't see much detail about him, but the look on my editor's face said he definitely appealed to her.

"Mr. Lockland, this is Megan Bradshaw, AKA Montana Raine." Kaitlin smiled for a brief second, and when I turned my head, I could see why.

Dark brown hair and silvery-blue eyes bewitched me, everything else in the room fading away. I swallowed hard, remembering my mother's words about being rude. I couldn't help it. He had the face and body of a model, perfect for the Abercrombie and Fitch catalogues, advertising sex on a stick.

When he stood, my gaze glided over his body. From his tight blue dress shirt, free from the tie he'd thrown on the couch next to him, to his long lean legs encased in black slacks—he practically made my mouth water. I wondered what was hidden from my viewing pleasure. My eyes shifted to the huge bulge between his legs, answering my question. I tried to keep my reaction to myself, but my throat clammed up as he spoke to me. It took me three tries before I could speak. I moved the necessary steps to shake hands with him.

"It's a pleasure to meet you, Mr. Lockland." I felt like a total idiot. I knew I blushed because he saw me staring. There was no way he could have missed it or my reaction.

A small quirk of his lips hinted at a smile, as his big hand engulfed mine. *Don't stare into his eyes*, I scolded myself. *Don't grip his hand too tight. And for Heaven's sake, do not stare at the incredible package between his thighs.* While my mind blundered the random thoughts of what I shouldn't do, he brought my hand to his mouth, kissing it with soft, warm lips.

A bolt of heat shot up my arm and went straight to my crotch, moisture pooling at my pussy lips. That lump in my throat came back—or maybe it had never really left—and I swallowed hard, my over-active imagination taking over again.

"The pleasure really is mine." His thumb rotated in small circles on the back of my hand.

I nearly came undone just thinking about that thumb stroking somewhere a little bit lower. With perfect pressure, he held my eyes with his, as if he knew the reaction he caused in my body. Maybe he was imagining it himself.

"Uh, if you'll excuse me, I need to get back to my table." Kaitlin cleared her throat, reminding us we weren't the only ones in the room.

Mr. Lockland looked over at her with a dismissing gesture. "Thanks Kaitlin. I'll inform you on the business side of the agreement tomorrow at our meeting."

She smiled, shifting her gaze to our interlocked hands. "Of course."

When she was gone, his glittering eyes returned to mine. "Have a seat." He pointed to the couch he'd occupied. "Can I get you something to drink?"

"No, thank you," I said minding my manners — making my momma proud — for the first time in my life. "Kaitlin said you wanted to talk to me about a book deal?"

His blue shirt accentuated his tanned skin, while his spicy cologne worked havoc on my senses. Was the room getting hot? Or was it just me? My breath hitched a bit, and I licked my lips to distract myself. Dammit! If he wasn't staring at me — my mouth — no doubt thinking things he'd rather being doing than talking business.

His gaze slowly lifted to meet my eyes. "Yes. I read your last novel and would like to offer you a five-book deal if you'll continue to write for Quicksand Books." He stood with his hands on his hips, his crotch straight in my line of vision, even though he stood several feet from me.

Maybe if he came a little closer and gave me a little taste, I'd consider. I chuckled. Who the hell was I kidding? Authors struggle to sell books. No matter how famous you are, it doesn't mean every book you write will be as great as the last. Ideally it should be better, but shit happens. Life gets in the way of your muse, and the next thing you know, you've contracted a deadly case of writer's block that threatens to end your career. Five books was a lot for a person with no general inspiration.

I'd just have to get inspired. Maybe I'd take a holiday on a cruise or something. Fellow writers say the Caribbean is the perfect place to see new things while being peaceful enough to find your muse. It was worth a try.

"Five books?" I smiled. "Wow. You like my writing that much?"

Blake stared at me. At first sight, I'd wanted his cock inside me, making it hard to have a serious conversation with him — a business conversation — without thinking of stripping him down and have him fuck me every way his imagination invented.

"Yes, I do." He cleared his throat, looking almost in pain. "You're last book, uh, was an interesting read. Possibly the highest selling digital book we've had since Quicksand Books opened its door five years ago. I haven't looked at the current paperback sales but judging by how many people have come by your table, I know they're grand as well."

If he'd read my book, from cover to cover, no wonder he was having a difficult time having a decent conversation with me. I wasn't ashamed. I just hated when men looked at me and expected me to do the things I'd made my characters do.

"I appreciate the deal, Mr. Lockland. I'd like to take you up on it." I stood. The conversation was over. Time for me get back to my table before someone complained. It had never happened to me but people can be annoyingly rude sometimes.

"Thank you." I extended my hand, uncomfortable with the way he stared at it. "If you'll have Kaitlin pass the contract to me that'll be great."

He took my hand in his again, spreading his warmth across my body. "Do you have any plans tonight, Megan? Or would you rather be called Montana? How'd you get that name anyway?"

Oh, Lordy, this man was working a real number on me. Back when I watched superhero movies, I remember special villains who had the power to suck energy out of the good guys with one touch. Not that he was a villain, but Blake

Lockland did that to me right now. The longer I was in a room with him the dirtier my thoughts became and the more willing I became to give into my temptation. Business was always separate from pleasure. *Always.*

"Um, I'm supposed to go shopping with my friends later," I replied, feeling stupid. "As for my name, I'm Megan to everyone that knows me. Montana is just for my fans." I avoided that last question. He didn't need to know about my stripper cousin giving me Montana as my stripping name. I decided to keep that information private.

"Okay, Megan. I have the contract ready. Perhaps I can bring it by personally, maybe over dinner tonight?" How could I resist? My thighs were drenched with my essence due to lack of underwear I didn't have the decency to put on. With one look from Blake, it was beyond me how I'd keep myself in check.

"Dinner? Um, I was sort of planning a quiet night at my hotel," I lied. "I'm working on a project, and I'm right in the middle of the first draft." *Yeah, planning the first draft maybe – God I hope he doesn't ask to read it.* "But I guess you can drop by the contract."

There's a bright idea, Megan. He thinks you're a slut and you just invited him to your hotel. What the hell had happened to my brain cells? He looked amused, finally releasing my hand.

"Ok, shall we make it seven?"

"Seven it is." I smiled, hoping he saw it as nothing more than that but doubting it all the same.

By the time I got back to my table the line filled the hall again, making my next few hours busier than I could imagine, which was good. The work kept my mind off Blake, and how he planned to come to my room tonight. If only it could distract my body the same way.

Chapter Two

I desperately tried to force myself to sit at my laptop and type something—anything—that resembled a story idea. The only thing I came up with was Blake coming to my hotel room and fucking my brains out.

Yeah, okay my pussy was needy. I couldn't help it. After being in a relationship for so long I'd gotten used to some things and it was hard to give them up. Maybe I was a sex addict and this was my withdrawal? No. That wasn't it. I hadn't even had the urge for six months after the breakup—until had Kaitlin introduced me to the handsome new owner of Quicksand Books.

Now, my pussy craved him. His fingers, his tongue, his cock—I wanted all of him. I laughed at the words I'd typed, my fingers quick to delete them. I really didn't need to think about fucking him. Sign the contract and get him out of my hotel room unscathed—that was my plan. No touching. No lingering looks of lust. No bodily reaction to his eyes, his mouth or his crotch. I would simply keep my hands, my eyes and my thoughts to myself.

A knock sounded at my door, and my heart jumped into my throat. Who was I kidding? Expecting him, knowing he looked undeniably handsome on the other side of my door, was enough to get me wet. The damn man didn't even have to be in the same room with me and I was drenched. God, how was I going to make it through a couple of minutes of close quarter contact?

I opened the door to a smiling man with Chinese food and a briefcase in his hands. I'd changed from my simple skirt and frilly camisole to plain lounging pants that could double for pyjamas and a white tank.

"You didn't have to bring food." I opened the door slightly, unable to hide my smile of appreciation.

"You wanted a quiet night in the hotel room, so I brought you dinner so you wouldn't be disturbed. How's the story coming along?"

I stepped aside allowing him to enter my hotel.

"Not good." I closed the door and went to the sofas in the centre of my suite. Blake was already there spreading out the food on the small coffee table. "I sort of have a bad case of writer's block."

I mentally thumped my head with my palm, thinking he'd withdraw my contract opportunity. It wasn't wise on my part to tell the owner of the publishing house I write for that my muse was gone. Not until after he gave me a nice contract offer, that is.

"Really?" He wadded the white paper sack, set it on the corner of the table, and squeezed between the sofa and coffee table, sitting on the floor. "I'm sure you'll get past it. Does it happen often?"

I scooted beside him, shrugging. "I've never had real writer's block until six months ago when I found out my boyfriend was cheating on me. You probably don't want to hear my dirty laundry."

He helped me open the containers. My mouth watered at the sweet and sour chicken and rice laid out before me. How had he known this was my favourite Chinese meal? I breathed in the sweet scent, my stomach growling from denial of food.

"You do like sweet and sour chicken, right?" He handed me an egg roll that I politely refused.

"Yes. It's the only thing Chinese I'll eat."

He held two fortune cookies putting one above my carton of food and one above his on the table.

It was ridiculous to smile at such a simple gesture. The guy bought me food—my favourite food, no less—and was actually being sweet. That was rare in my experience. The last time a man had treated me to a meal was the first night Rich had asked me out. From then on it had been fend for myself.

"I can see those wheels turning." He smiled, biting into an egg roll. "What's going through your mind?"

Other than the fact I feel like an idiot? Nothing. "I'm just curious as to why you want to give me a five book contract?"

I ate, revelling in the delicious taste of the chicken. For a brief moment, I forgot about my muse, my life, my sexual appetite—I forgot about everything. The food slid down the back of my throat slowly burning with its spicy flavour as he stared at me.

"You're a writer. I'm a publisher. You write great books. I want to sell your books." He shrugged. "Plus I liked you the moment I saw you. I've read your book, your biography and even Googled your website to learn as much about you as I could. I want to work with you, Megan. That's the reason I offered you the contract."

And here I was thinking dirty thoughts about him and his amazing cock. He was being totally professional towards me and I was acting like a horny sex-withdrawn slut ready to open my legs for the first dick that came walking by. What the hell had I been thinking?

The rest of the meal was mostly business. He pulled out the contract and explained the fine print. We negotiated royalties and advances. Since Quicksand Books is mostly a digital publisher, the only advances they pay are for series. He offered me the opportunity to write for one of the up-coming series, but I declined. I'm not one for people telling me what or how to write.

Blake remained completely professional, so unlike any other male I'd met before him. I will not brag about my looks, but several have said they found me attractive. Blonde hair, big boobs—I'm a walking cliché of a life size Barbie, but I do have a brain. I earned my MBA in less than half the time I was permitted, while taking creative writing classes on the side. I hardly ever bragged about anything but my books. My books I can't talk enough about.

"So, you're next signing is at the Chicago conference?" Blake seemed all too happy about that.

Quicksand Books, Inc. was located in the heart of the magnificent Windy City. I'd put my sexual attraction for him on hold because he was being all professional and everything. I didn't know what he was hinting at now, but if it was to invite me to do anything with him, I'd have to decline.

"Yes," I said, wishing I had a better distraction than cleaning up the remnants of our meal. "Why?"

He studied me, causing pause in my actions. I stood with my hands on my hips—the best defence I had—staring down at him. Okay, I tried my damndest to be a bad ass when in reality I cared more than I wanted to.

"I like you, Megan. I want to see you again."

If that wasn't a shock nothing was. "Like a date?"

He chuckled. "Yes. Like a date."

I stared at him for a long moment, certain parts of my body screaming one thing, while my brain said another. His eyes were cool and mesmerising, and my body heat rose a notch. I thought I'd been unreasonable in thinking dirty little thoughts about what I wanted him to do. My pussy responded at my memory. Now, maybe I wasn't so wrong.

"Like a relationship or just a fuck?" Maybe I sounded a little bitchy, but guys did this all the time when they found out what I do for a living. They seemed to think writing about sexy people doing sexy things means the writer does all those things in real life. I hated being compared to my characters.

He stood, probably feeling slightly disadvantaged sitting on the floor with me narrowing my eyes at him, but I didn't care. I'd already signed the contract, so technically I didn't have to kiss his ass.

"What do you want, Megan?" He seemed cool and collected, mocking my stance with his hands on his hips. "Do you want a true relationship or just a fuck?"

Right now? Fucking wins. "Why does it matter what I want? I'm asking your intentions. This isn't the first time a man has read my work then tried to get into my panties to see if I do half the stuff I write about. And if that is your intention you'll get a fast rejection because I'm not putting up with it."

I really didn't want it to be his intention, but I had to find out. Men are fickle creatures who hold more mysteries than a Stephen King novel. I stared into his eyes as he contemplated my response.

"I'm sorry some losers have made you feel that way, but that's not my intention. Yeah, I'm attracted to you. Yes, my cock responds to you. Any red-blooded male with a beating heart would."

I felt like a moron. "I'm sorry. I didn't mean to accuse you."

"I accept your apology." He dropped his hands to his side. "Now, answer my question."

"Do I want sex? Yes." I looked away, contemplating my next move.

He stepped around the coffee table, pulling me against him. The hard wall of his chest slammed against my breasts with full force as he lowered his mouth to mine. The taste of the sweet and sour sauce lingered on his tongue along with the flavour of hot, desirable male and a taste that was unique to Blake Lockland.

He licked at my mouth, his lips a sweet caress against my own. I sucked gently on his probing tongue, as I wrapped my arms around his neck. His steely cock pressed into my stomach as he gripped my ass, pulling me closer. He lifted me slightly until the sweet pleasure of our bodies rubbing against each other created pooling moisture between my thighs.

"Tell me now if you want this to stop." His breaths came in hot short bursts of air in my face.

"No. Don't stop, Blake."

Somehow, the whole undressing thing, blurred in my mind. Miraculously our clothes flew from our bodies and landed in piles leading from the couch to where we stood next to the bed. Blake's mouth was hot on mine, his hands touching everywhere.

The man worshiped my breasts, his fingers rolling my nipples until they pebbled. I moaned against his mouth and he responded by doing it again. His tongue lashed out licking my nipple as if it was a creamy ice cream cone and he was burning up. I nearly came then and we hadn't even gotten started.

"Blake," I moaned as he kissed his way down my body. "Blake, I need…" The last of my thought faded when he slid the crotch of my panties aside and flicked my clit with the tip of his tongue.

Damn. If he hadn't been holding my hips firmly in his hands, I would have fallen on my ass. Thankfully, there was a bed behind me but that wasn't the point. His tongue flicked my pussy. The hungry need to have him inside me was overwhelming. My hands latched on to his short brown hair, keeping him where I needed him.

"I want you now," I said trying to pull him up. I was breathless and panting as he continued his sweet torture. I didn't want to come this way. I wanted him inside me. I wanted him to fuck me with his cock until I lost my voice from screaming. I wanted him to let me suck him like he sucked me, feeling the pulsing length of him in my mouth. "God, enough. Fuck me now!"

In an instant he stood, his mouth coming down hard against mine. The force of his body sent me crashing back on the mattress, his large body covering me. He still wore his boxers but his erection prodded my clit as if there were nothing between us. I felt him, the heat, the hardness and wanted him more.

"God, Meg." He pulled back long enough to get a condom out of his jeans pocket. "You taste so good."

He pulled his boxers down freeing his magnificent cock for my viewing pleasure and donned the condom in one quick move. I didn't have time to admire him before he shoved inside my pussy in one hard stroke. I stretched to accommodate him, but he was big. The kind of big magnum condoms were made for. Yeah, I never thought a man would really need the "magnum" size. I just figured every man had his dreams, and if buying a box of magnum sized condoms made him feel better, then so be it. Boy, was I wrong.

He stopped a minute, his blazing blue eyes dilated with arousal, almost black in the low light. "You're a fucking fist, Meg. God, are you always this tight?"

My six months of abstinence could have contributed to that problem, but he didn't need to know that. Instead I moaned and lifted my hips, pushing his steely length impossibly farther inside me.

Okay, I felt a smirk on my face when his eyes rolled in the back of his head, but as far as I was concerned, talking time was over. Now was the time for action. Hot, wild sexy action that ended with both of us panting and screaming.

He pulled out, nearly all the way and shoved right back in. Again it took a few seconds for my body to get used to his size and the movement. Each stroke held delightful friction, his cock hitting my G-spot perfectly. I felt moisture seep out of my body, when his mouth found my breasts again. My orgasm was coming, but I wanted to make it last. I didn't want the rhythmic strokes to cease. The pleasure was too great for me to ever want it to end.

"Let it go, baby," he said, his hot tongue licking a path to the pulsing vein in my neck. "Let it go and come for me."

His mouth slid to my breast, while his fingers found their way between our meshed bodies, fondling my clit. One stroke and I arched my back. Two strokes and I gasped. Three strokes and I fell apart. In the far distance I heard a scream, my pulse pounding hard in my ears. My body convulsed gripping him, squeezing him until he let out a string of curses as he came.

When we slowly drifted back down to earth, he rolled off me to take care of the condom. I couldn't move. My arms were limp, my thighs ached and the mind numbing serenity I felt was too good to disturb. Oh, I'd had sex before—plenty of it—but nothing like this. I'd never been fucked so...*amazingly*...and had an orgasm so powerful and tiring that I couldn't open my eyelids. I was completely sated.

When Blake came back, he crawled towards me, lying on his side staring at me. His hand stroked my stomach, the tip of his finger drawing circles around my navel.

"Is our sexual relationship going to be awkward for our working environment?" I wondered aloud.

"Not on my part. You?"

I finally mustered up enough energy to turn to face him. "Depends. Is this a one night thing or is this something a little bit more?"

His hand stilled, pressing his palm flat against my belly. I wasn't sure if I wanted it to be more, yet here I was pressing him for answers. How insensitive was that of me? I pulled his hand up with mine, linking our fingers together. Maybe he wouldn't answer. Maybe me and my big fat mouth would learn how to keep my lips shut.

"It'll be hard having a relationship living in two different cities, across the country from each other," he finally said, his eyes locking with mine.

Okay. That's fine. I knew in the back of my mind this was a one-night stand. But that didn't mean it hurt any less to be rejected. "Yeah."

I felt vulnerable and exposed lying naked next to this man with our fingers interlocked. God, I was an emotional wreck. I'd had meaningless sex encounters where we stripped, fucked and put our clothes back on ending the night with a trusty "thank you for that wonderful orgasm." I'd been there.

I'd done that. So why the hell was I getting all worked up over this man? He'd told me the same thing many guys before him had told me. Why did I feel he was different?

"Meg, what's wrong?" He sat up, hovering over me.

"Nothing." I felt stupid again. Dammit if the dumb blonde euphuism wasn't alive and well tonight. I sat up, pushing him back against the mattress. I needed my clothing. There was no way in hell I was going to walk across the room butt-naked. Yeah, he'd seen every part of me, but still. It felt weird, especially in a hotel.

I grabbed his shirt instead to wrap around my body until I got my own clothes.

"Meg, tell me what's wrong." He pushed up, propping his exceptional body up with his arms.

"I think we should remain on a professional level," I said pulling my pants on with my back turned away from him. "It'll be easier that way."

"Fuck easy. What made you sullen all of a sudden?" He stood as I pulled off his shirt and turned me around to face him, breasts exposed. "Just because we live apart doesn't mean we don't have a fighting chance. Meg—hell I don't know what I want but I feel something special with you. I can't say that's the foundation to a lasting relationship, but I want to explore it."

I rolled my eyes, oblivious to my nakedness. "Look, Blake, you're off the hook. You don't have to feel sorry for me. It was consensual sex."

He pushed me back against the wooden bedpost, slight pain biting at my back. "You might want this to be a one night stand, but what about what I want? Are you so shallow to believe men can't have real feelings for women?"

Real feelings—no. Expressing feelings—that's a different story. I stared into his eyes, hating the way my body responded to him. I knew I should stick to my guns and ignore what he said. I should kick him out of my hotel room and never think about him again...only he was the owner of the company where I'd just signed a five book contract.

Dammit. I was fucked over again.

"Meg, you try hiding your heart behind worthless barriers that I'm only going to tear down." A wicked gleam sparkled in his eyes. "Keep trying sweetheart, I like the challenge."

Before I conjured a response, he pulled on his clothes and headed out of my hotel room and out of my life. The last sight of him was his very fine ass, sculpted to perfection, leaving me...

Chapter Three

Chicago, Illinois

Three weeks and no sign from Blake.

Ever since our romp in the hotel room, followed by our fight, I hadn't so much as heard anything from the owner of Quicksand Books. Kaitlin called me to see if I'd signed the contract. I'd told her I had. Nothing more was said, nothing more was done.

Now I sat at my table at the convention autographing my book for adoring fans and he walked into the room. I thought I'd be pissed to see him, but my body reacted to his memory, making my job harder now that he stood in the same room. Groaning, I put on a fake smile as I greeted my fans.

I avoided his gaze though I felt his eyes on me as a woman asked if she could take a picture. Of course I said yes. I'd been writing some in my little breaks — just to clear my head if nothing else. Granted, I wouldn't claim he'd given me my muse back, but he had helped with the tension blocking my creativity.

"Ms. Raine, I'm such a huge fan," a younger woman proclaimed as she came up to me. "I have every one of your books and how-to articles. I'm an aspiring author, myself."

I grinned. "That's lovely. What's your name, so when you get published I can make sure to buy a copy of your book?" It most likely wasn't going to happen since half the people who proclaim they want to be writers have yet to complete a first draft.

"Bethany. Bethany Miller," she said happily. "It's sensual romance too. About a…"

As she continued, I couldn't help shifting my gaze to the man staring at me. I wanted to send him a hateful look, but he had a smile on his face—a devastatingly perfect smile that made me think twice. What the hell was wrong with me?

He started for my table as I shifted my attention back to the woman. I couldn't really make sense of her conversation about her book, but I tried my damndest to keep my thoughts on her instead of the man now standing beside me.

I hated feelings like this. The nervousness for no reason, the sudden arousal at the memories of what had happened, and the stupidity that followed my really bad decision—I felt them all right now and suspected they wouldn't go away any time soon.

"…So that's my book. I'm still working on the first draft but I plan to be sending it out soon. I just hope editors will think it's good enough to buy." Bethany shifted her gaze to Blake and smiled. "Hi. I'm Bethany."

He smiled back, the prick. "Nice to meet you, Bethany. Did I hear you're writing a book?"

If he'd turned up the charm any more, I might have puked all over the paperback books situated on the table before me. I started signing another lady's book hoping that Bethany would soon end her non-stop chatter and move about the conference with the rest of the people visiting. But no. She was hitting on Mr. Charming trying to get him to buy her book. *Please, how unprofessional.*

I listened with a strained ear to their conversation while my fans continuously praised my work and gushed about how much they loved my writing. I'm grateful, truly I am, but other things mattered more at the moment. Especially things I couldn't concentrate on hearing.

My line shortened and Bethany finally left. Mr. Charming however stood in place next to me with his hand on my folding chair. "Nice girl," he commented when the line finally ended. I think perhaps everyone who'd come to the conference had bought my book. If not, it would have shocked to me.

"Yeah. A true bimbo," I commented, bending down to get my water bottle from my bag. I unscrewed the cap and took a drink to wet my parched throat. I replaced the cap and dropped the water bottle back in my bag. In Atlanta, Blake had asked me if I wanted a relationship. I'd thought about it and my answer was no. I didn't or at least I didn't think I did.

"Bethany seemed nice, not like a bimbo." He squatted down beside me, keeping his hand on the back of my chair. "We need to talk."

"No. *We* don't," I corrected, smiling as two women gave us wondering glances. "You go about your business, and I'll go about mine."

His hand stroked my thigh. "You are my business."

Okay, I should have been offended. The guy was touching me in public and calling me his business. Yes, I know I write for his company, but I wasn't and didn't claim to be anybody's anything.

I cursed myself for wearing a cute black mini-skirt that showed off my freshly waxed legs. Smooth, as a baby's behind, is what the Chinese lady had said about me. Now I wished I had on denim jeans and a turtleneck sweater. Though, even that couldn't prevent the reaction I had to Blake.

His finger continued to tantalise me, working its way to the hem of my skirt underneath the table. Clearly in plain view, we looked as if we were having a normal conversation. As long as I kept my reaction to his wandering finger hidden, no one would notice anything abnormal.

"What do you want, Mr. Lockland?" I asked trying to remain professional. I grabbed his hand before his nimble fingers slid to my crotch.

"I wanted to ask you over to my place," he said, his gaze intent, waiting for my reaction.

"Sorry stud, but I have a hotel room." I turned, keeping my hand wrapped around his, just in case he started to get frisky again, while I signed another fan's book. I made my polite thank-yous and turned back to his amused face. "What?"

"Stop being stubborn and come over." Using the hand that we had locked together, he gripped my thigh before I could stop him. Delicious tremors of heat found their way to my pussy. "I'll take you out to eat then show you around the city a little bit."

"No," I said. He started massaging my thigh, running his fingers lightly over my soft skin, and I lost all reasoning. It was all I could do not to open my legs farther and put his hand where I wanted it to be.

"Yes," he countered, sliding his hand away from my body. "This thing is over in two hours. Meet me out front at eight."

As he stood, he leaned forward slightly and anyone who watched would have seen his lips grace my temple. If they studied my expression, they'd have known his finger pressed against my clit, sending delicious tremors throughout my body.

I watched him go about his business over at the Quicksand Books table, charming the pants off hopeful aspiring authors. Any girl would be crazy — or gay — not to be attracted to him. He normally wore suits, I noticed, or dress clothes. I couldn't help remembering — and picturing in my mind — what he'd looked like in jeans.

The next two hours were pure hell. I had maybe three fans looking at my book, several old women sticking their noses up at me and two men who looked at me as if I were a piece of ass. I was alone at my booth this time and had to ward off the contentious requests for my phone number. I even had a guy ask me if I was a prostitute who'd do the things I write about if he paid me. Security escorted him away from my table.

"Hey," Blake said coming up behind me. "What's the deal with security?"

"I've had a really bad night," I said trying to keep it together. "I just want to go back to my hotel room and sulk."

He stared at me, but I avoided his gaze.

"Okay. You want to tell me what happened?" Blake asked. Outside it was pouring down rain, and I contemplated whether or not I could make it to my car without being soaked. Granted it was a rental, and I hated to admit it, but I couldn't remember which Ford Taurus it was. There were five parked in the same general area where I'd parked, all of the same colour. Too bad the key chain didn't have keyless entry like my Mercedes. I'd find that baby in a heartbeat.

"A guy just gave me the creeps," I said still looking out into the parking lot. "He asked me if I would do the stuff I wrote about to him if he paid me."

Blake didn't say anything, so I turned to see if he was still there. He was, only his jaw was set and anger shown in his eyes. He was pissed.

"Look, it's not that big of a deal. I'll go home, take a shower and get back to my life." I shrugged. "I'd have figured you'd know about this type of crap since you publish what I write."

He pulled me to him, his long arms wrapping around my body. "I'm sorry you have to deal with that."

"Yeah, me too." I pulled away from his embrace. "I know I might sound like a dumb blonde right now, but I can't remember which green Taurus is my rental."

He laughed, hands on his hips, shaking his head. "Then I guess you'll have to ride with me, huh?"

"You're sly, I'll give you that." Instead of fighting him, I went with it.

He told me to stay there while he went to get his car. I couldn't help smiling at the gentlemanly offer, considering I was going to get wet anyhow.

I sprinted to his car where he held open the passenger door. He shut me in, and just as I'd expected I looked as if I'd walked into a sprinkler system. Blake climbed in the driver's seat looking as if he'd taken a swim in his Armani suit. He didn't seem to care too much though. He turned on the heat to fight against the chill, and before I knew it, we arrived at a fancy apartment building. I should have known better than to think he'd drive me to my hotel.

"You know I pinned you for a nice guy," I said as we drove through the parking structure. "But I'm starting to reconsider that opinion since you brought me back to your place for God knows what." I knew what he brought me back here for and it wasn't simply because he wanted to show me his big screen TV. And surprising me the most, I was kind of excited.

"I am a nice guy," he said, wicked intent showing in his eyes. "Otherwise you wouldn't be here."

He parked and led me to the back of the structure where the elevators led us to the apartments in the tall building above. His was on floor twenty-three, ironically apartment 23C.

At first glance I thought he'd brought me to Oprah's place. The fancy decorations surprised me for a bachelor's pad. It was nicely toned in leather and neutral colours. Blue livened up the place, with decorative artwork hanging on the walls. A plasma TV hung on the wall with a very nice stereo with large speakers on each side of the entertainment centre.

"Wow," was the only word that came to mind.

He smiled. "It's just stuff, Meg. You want something to drink? Some clothes to change into? Are you hungry?"

"Clothes please," I said afraid to step on his very expensive looking rug.

"All right." He stripped off his jacket, tie and shoes, leaving them in the foyer. He continued pulling off his shirt as he talked. "I'm not sure what I have in the kitchen to eat but we can always order takeout if you're hungry."

The sight of his broad naked chest sent a fresh burst of desire through me. I'd seen it before. I'd felt him before. And I wanted him again. I swallowed my thoughts, hoping he didn't notice as I too took off my shoes. I didn't wear a jacket, and I knew my nipples betrayed me through my thin shirt, but I ignored it.

He smiled, staring at me and causing my body to react. "Why are you nervous? It's not like I'm going to jump you."

"No but I might you..." I mumbled turning away from him. "Have you always lived in Chicago?"

I heard his zipper and turned to see him shredding the last of his clothing in the foyer before me. What kind of defence would I have if he stood naked and I was hot and bothered, fully clothed? He looked up at me, and I nearly giggled like a schoolgirl. Dammit.

"What? You've seen me naked before." His smug smile charmed me nonetheless. "If memory serves, you liked it a lot."

My cheeks heated. "Go get clothes."

He shook his head and turned his nicely tanned behind, to strut down the hall. A few seconds later, he returned wearing long basketball shorts and held a large tee for me.

"Bathroom?" I asked, not nearly as bold as him.

He scoffed, rolling his eyes. "Women." He pointed towards the hall he'd come from. "Any one of those rooms is fine to change. Bathroom is second door on the right."

I trotted to the bathroom, flipping on the bright overhead light. The decadent blue room held the bare necessities for me to work with. My mascara blackened my eyes, making me look like a raccoon. There was a soft towel though that I used to dry my wet hair. Other than that, I had to go as I was. I slipped off my clothes, ringing them out in the sink then neatly hanging them over the shower rod. The shirt he'd given me barely came to mid-thigh, and I suddenly realised he'd done that on purpose. The only thing of mine I wore was my thong, and that was more of a necessity than anything — though it didn't cover much.

I took one last look in the mirror and unlocked the door only to run right into Blake's hard chest. His hands clamped on my shoulders to steady me, but my legs threatened to give out. What was it with this man?

"Whoa. You okay?" His smile was warm and I almost wished I could plaster a frown across my lips.

"Peachy." I needed something to cover my lower body. "Do you have any shorts I can borrow?"

"Meg, really?" He looked at me like I was joking. "I ordered pizza. I need to take care of a few things, so if he comes would you please give him the money I left on the foyer table. It should only take a second, but it's an important business call."

"I'm not answering the door wearing a T-shirt and showing half my ass!" I screeched "Are you insane? Pizza boys are horny enough as it is."

He started laughing, and I grew more pissed. I think he could tell, because he laughed harder. I tried to pull from his grip, but he pulled me closer. His lips were mere inches from mine and it seemed the world stopped turning. He stopped laughing, and I forgot what the hell had me so pissed. I knew he wanted to kiss me, and Lord, I wanted him to just as much.

I leaned forward first, brushing my lips against his. There was a spark of recognition through my body that had my pussy aching in a matter of seconds. The memories of his hands on my body, the way his lips felt against my breasts — I wanted him again.

He pulled back first, dropping his hands to his side and clenching his fists. "I thought you didn't want a relationship?"

"How could I not when it's with you?" I was a hypocrite in my own mind. I loved the attention he gave me, and honestly I think I would have dated him if we hadn't met under the circumstances we had. He treated me nicely, like I was worth more than a good fuck and even though the sex was awesome, magnificent, wonderful, he didn't make me feel worthless or coerced like Rich had.

"So are we seeing each other?" he asked, his eyes studying mine.

"Can we? I mean does company policy allow your girlfriend to be one of your contracted authors?" I leaned against the closed bathroom door, needing strength to have this conversation with him. I hated talking about the future — especially when I didn't even know what I wanted. Rich had been my future for so long. It had been hard for me to get back on my own two feet and start to live again. "I'll be honest, I don't want a relationship like the one I came out of. Rich was more than controlling and it took me seven years to realise it. I played with fire and got burned."

His hand came up to my face. "Rich sounds like a prick."

He kissed me again, sweet and tender but no less passionate. I had no intention of putting my heart on the line again. Yeah, I liked men, and I liked sex, but I didn't want to be tied down to anyone. I don't like being controlled.

"We'll finish more of this later," he said pulling away, rubbing his thumb across my bottom lip. "I'll get you a pair of boxers to wear, how is that?"

Fine, I assumed. It's not like I really wanted to answer the door wearing his boxers and tee but I supposed it was better than just wearing the tee. I followed him to his bedroom, gasping at the huge bed that sat on a small platform in the centre of the room. Blue sheets covered the mattress on the massive king-sized wooden bed. It was the sort of thing a girl could fall back on and revel in the softness against her skin.

"Here." He slung the shorts at me, smiling as he caught my mouth opened, staring at his bed. "Do you like my room?"

I nodded dumbly. "Does this whole 'new relationship' thing involve me sleeping there?"

"Yes," he said moving past me to grab his phone. "Now put those on and get out of here so I can get this over with."

I narrowed my eyes, "That's a bit rude."

"Go." He pointed to the door, smile still on his face.

I licked my lips, hiking the shirt up to my waist as I pulled off my turquoise thong, watching his eyes dilate the whole time. My pussy contracted when his gaze lingered on my crotch. The smile left his face, and pure raw passion took its place. I bent down allowing the shirt to cover most of me and picked up my underwear. I flicked it at him, like a slingshot, hitting him square in the chest. He caught it before it fell to the floor, our little game taking a different turn.

"Was that payback for being rude?" he asked, wrapping his hand around my underwear.

"No," I said stepping into the boxers he'd given me. "I'm just changing."

"Just killing me, is what you're doing."

I glanced at his body. His shorts were tenting as he stood before me, slowly rubbing my thong in his hand.

"Fine. I'll leave you alone. Don't be long though." I left without another word.

I waited impatiently on the black leather sofa for the stupid pizza boy. The apartment was too quiet. I thought about watching TV but it'd be rude of me to just make myself at home without the proper invitation. So I sat and waited until Blake came back from his bedroom.

"No pizza?" He kissed my head as he walked past the sofa.

"Nope. I think he got lost."

He walked around the sofa, plopping down next to me then taking my feet in his hands. He rested them in his lap while he began to massage, his fingers erasing the pain my four inch heels caused. I'd never gotten a foot massage from a guy, mainly because I'm ticklish, but Blake had wonderful hands that knew exactly what I wanted them to do. I leaned back, closing my eyes and enjoying his touch.

"I like your pink toes," he said, his voice warm and husky.

"Courtesy of my favourite nail technician," I mumbled, my whole body relaxing. "Did your business thing go okay?"

"Yep. My sister officially said that I own half the company. I'm the one who will be making the decisions instead of her."

I opened my eyes, sitting up and drawing my foot away from him. "Wow. Are you going to edit and stuff like she did?"

He pulled my foot back. "No. I'm not an editor, but I will read and have the final say on which stories my editors think we should print. I'll say if someone is to be accepted or rejected."

"Oh, so now I have to woo you?" I leaned my head back against the couch, closing my eyes with a smile. The man had great hands.

"You already woo me," he said, pushing my foot aside. He urged me down against the couch, his hard body pressing against mine, while his amazing hands sought the empty place where I wanted him to be. "Evidently I woo you too."

He kissed me, while he plunged two fingers inside my body, I moaned into his mouth, a sound he appreciated as he moved his long, slick fingers in and out of my pussy. The doorbell buzzed announcing the arrival of the pizza boy but neither one of us reacted in haste. When Blake finally did pull his mouth from mine, he took his fingers away too, bringing them to his lips to lick them clean.

"Stay here," he said, standing. He disappeared for a few seconds then came back with a large pizza and a box of cinnamon bread.

Whoever knew Chicago could be so fun?

Chapter Four

After dinner, everything blurred. One minute we were eating pizza, and the next my clothes were flying across the room. Somehow Blake carried me to his bedroom and laid me across that magnificent bed, soft as a cloud in the sky. His mouth covered mine as he pushed my thighs apart, feeling how wet I was for him.

"I want to fuck you now," he said against my mouth.

I was beyond telling him no. "Go for it, big boy."

I arched my hips just as he thrust forward. Even though my last sexual escapade had involved him and had only been three weeks ago, I had to give my body time to adjust to his size. He held still understanding, using the time to tenderly kiss my breasts while his fingers stroked my stomach.

When he started moving his hips, I sucked in much needed air into my lungs. The sweet friction of the rhythmic stroking of his cock as it slid in and out built my climax rapidly. It didn't take long until I was there. I screamed digging my nails into his back, sliding them down to grip his ass and push him deeper inside me.

His mouth latched on to my breast, sucking my nipple. I came again without warning, this time arching my back off the mattress. When the final waves receded, he pulled out and away from me, staring down. His cock was still hard and wet from my moisture.

"Turn over," he said, his eyes gleaming with wicked intent. "I want to fuck you from behind."

For a brief second, I wasn't sure I could move. After a few seconds of silence and mild debate I figure what the hell. I turned over. He slid into me again and I screamed at the contact. The new angle felt amazing hitting my G-spot while the continuous slide of in and out had me coming. I smiled to myself, squeezing him with my inner walls. He pumped faster and harder. My muscles screamed from strain until finally he came, pulling me over with him again.

I couldn't move, even when he rolled off me. My body relaxed to the point my limbs felt like spaghetti.

"How do you do that?" Blake asked

I gained enough strength through curiosity to turn my head and look at him. He lay on his back with a wrist thrown across his face. A small smile played on his lips. He looked peaceful. Relaxed.

"Do what?" I asked my head swimming due to lack of oxygen to my brain.

"Turn me on. I'm hard just thinking about you five seconds after I come." He rolled over, brushing a piece of hair off my face, before he kissed my cheek. "I could have sex with you all night long, you know, and never tire."

"Oh?" I rolled over yawning before facing him again. "I'm just good at what I do."

He chuckled. "That you are."

I knew in my mind that this guy was too good to be true. After sex, he wanted to hold me in his bed. He suggested we watch a movie—my choice of course—until we gained enough strength for round two. I told him four orgasms in one night were plenty for me, but he mockingly replied, he had some catching up to do.

We decided to take a shower, where I gave him a little sample of some of my other talents. He wanted to even the score? Fine by me. We crammed into his fancy—yet, small—shower stall, where I knelt and took him into my mouth. I thought he was big for my body, but good lord, that was nothing compared for my mouth.

I pumped him mostly with my fist, while attentively sucking the head of his cock. He instructed me on how he liked it, and I complied. I felt him holding back his orgasm when he nearly pulled my wet hair from my scalp. I pushed him farther in my mouth, sucking harder, silently telling him to let it go, just like he did for me our first night together.

He came in a hot burst of pleasure, coating my tongue and throat with his warm, salty fluid. The water had turned cold now, and I was damn near freezing, yet burning up inside all at the same time. I kissed the tip of him once more before pulling back to stare up at his placid body. He was beautiful, standing there completely sated like a magnificent Greek statue, with his eyes closed and his receding tremors barely noticeable.

I stood up, flicked off the cold spray and grabbed two towels from the rack. I dried him off while he remained still.

"You can move now," I said, standing on tiptoe to peck his cheek.

His arms came around my waist as he buried his face in my neck. "Thank you. God, you're wonderful." He pulled back, pushing my hair from my face. "What did I ever do to deserve you?"

I didn't have an answer for that. Instead I considered the question rhetorical and kissed him. He lifted me into his arms, towel half hanging on me, half touching the floor and carried me back to his bed. He bent over me, smiling. It wasn't an "up to something" kind of smile. It was more of an "I'm happy you're here" kind of smile.

"Do you want to watch a movie or go to sleep?" he asked looking over at the clock.

It was well past midnight, so I figured we'd better sleep. We could spare a few hours to catch some Zs. "Sleep."

He left only to turn out the light and came back, stripping the towels from both our bodies. He crawled in next to me, wrapping the covers around us, as he cradled me against his body. It was a loving gesture that had my emotions in an even bigger frenzy. If he kept doing stuff like this, I was going to fall in love with him. Then where would I be?

* * * *

Blake woke me up at five, his protruding cock prodding my backside. I smiled once I recognised where I was. The rain outside beat softly against the windows the rising sun casting a soft glow of light into his room. *It's impossible for us to be this horny*, I thought, slipping my hand back to touch him.

The moment my fingers curled around him, his body tensed, his erection growing longer and harder.

"Is that the way you normally wake your lovers in the morning?" he asked half awake.

"You woke me, big boy." I turned to capture his lips with a kiss. "Good morning."

"Meg, I've been thinking." He sat up, the covers falling down to his waist. "I sat up all night figuring out how this relationship is going to work. I want you to move in with me."

"What?" I shrieked. "Move in with you? That's a big step, Blake. Not to mention I live in North Carolina. What brought this on?"

"I don't want to lose you. I can't leave Chicago because of the company. You can write anywhere, right? You can move up here, and we can be together." If his face wasn't so cute, I'd have slapped him.

"Why should I have to be the one to make the sacrifices? I told you I didn't want another relationship like the one I had with Rich. He controlled me and used me, and I won't let another man do that to me, including you." I sat up clutching the sheet to my chest.

"I'm not trying to control or use you. I'm trying to figure out a way we can be together." He seemed dead serious as he stared at me.

"No, Blake. You're just like Rich. I don't want to live in Chicago. I like my little town in North Carolina just fine. I have a house by the ocean and I don't know how you can ask me to give up my life and move here."

I slid from the bed and ran to the bathroom, hating the fact tears were in my eyes. I wasn't going to cry. I changed back into the clothes I'd hung on the shower rod the night before and came back out to find Blake sitting on the couch, looking equally distraught as I felt. He'd donned a pair of jeans, and pulled the shirt I'd worn over his head.

Who was I kidding? A relationship would never come out of what we had. A relationship could never be based on sex, no matter how good one thought it might be.

"Can you take me back to my car?"

"Let's go," he said, grabbing his keys.

Those were the last words he said to me while I was in Chicago.

Chapter Five

Wilmington, North Carolina
Three months later...

I spent most of my days crying over what had happened in Chicago, mainly because I felt like a fool. I sulked, typing my heart out on my laptop as I sat on my back deck writing about the love I wished I had. I completed a rough first draft and sent it to Kaitlin for review, who sent it back with plenty revisions for me to work on.

The great thing about working with an electronic publisher was that everything was done through e-mail. I never had to print or mail or show up in person—except for a few rare instances. Nope, the whole world was at the tips of my fingers.

Blake called me once, but I didn't answer him. He said he knew I was pissed and that he wished I would talk to him about it. I clicked off my answering machine and plugged in my iPod. Enough with the real world crap; it was time to get down to business.

My fingers flew across the keyboard, correcting flaws Kaitlin had found in my manuscript. Granted it wasn't much, just a few odds and ends here and there. I typed until my hands risked carpel tunnel syndrome from the constant small movements of my wrists and fingers. I didn't care. I had five damn books to create and I was going to do it. I forced my butt in my seat and stared at the computer screen. Two down, three to go. Maybe then, when my contract was up, I'd consider seeking a new publisher.

Blake entered my mind again and an unexplainable sad sensation overwhelmed me. I didn't know what I wanted from him. A little part of me wanted him to chase after me and be the fantasy I'd desired for so long. But another part of me was furious he had even considered asking me to give up my life as I knew it to be with him.

I saw a shadow round the corner of my house. I stood ready to yell at the guy, when I saw who it was. My emotions caught in my throat as my heart twisted into a web of hurt, love and confusion.

"I rang the doorbell, but you didn't answer." Blake stood in his usual business suit, so unlike the look I'd last seen him wearing.

"I didn't hear it. I was busy creating stories and listening to my iPod." The polite thing to do would be invite him inside and offer him something to drink. Too bad I didn't feel like being polite.

"Meg, I was wrong," he blurted it without moving a muscle in his body. "I know I sounded crazy, and you think I was controlling or whatever but I...I want us to work."

"Blake, what are you doing here?" I sat down on the step, my heart skipping a beat.

"Meg, I'm trying here." He combed his fingers through his hair. "I told my sister that unless I could run the business from anywhere in the world, I wanted nothing to do with it. She told me to come after you and beg for your forgiveness then spend the rest of my life making it up to you." He finally stepped closer, sitting on the step next to me. "Meg, I'm sorry I asked you to give this up. I really didn't think about it thoroughly and just wanted so badly for us to find a way to be together."

I understood that. "So what are you saying?"

"I want to be with you. I can work from North Carolina, Texas, Georgia—wherever you want to go. I just want to be with you, no matter what city we're in."

I couldn't help but smile. Was this a fantasy? Or was this the reality a handful of people actually experienced once in their lifetime? Either way I couldn't stay mad at him for too long. He was here, and true to his word, making an effort. The least I could do was to give him an inch.

"I'm a moody writer. I don't get along well with others," I said. "Can you handle that?"

"I can handle anything you're willing to throw my way."

He pulled me to him and held me for a long time, sitting on my back deck. His body was warm and familiar. I'd never realised how much I missed him until then. I pulled back and stood up holding my hand out to him.

"Come on city boy, it's hot out here. Do you want some iced tea?" I picked up my laptop and carted it inside.

"Sure." He shrugged out of his suit coat and settled on one of the kitchen barstools. "Kaitlin said you sent her your latest manuscript. What's it about?"

I pulled it up on my computer. "Read while I pour our drinks."

I pulled two glasses from the cabinet, then filled them with ice cubes in the shape of little stars, courtesy of my summer collection of ice trays. I poured the tea, the ice crackling as the slightly warmer liquid hit it. When I turned around, Blake was staring at me. I knew he'd just finished reading part of what I'd written. Granted it wasn't the full manuscript, but it was enough of a sampler for him to get a taste.

"Do you like it?" I asked, handing him his glass.

He tipped the glass to his lips downing half of the contents in one gulp. Afterward he began undoing his shirt and tie. When he finally spoke he said, "You're one heck of a woman, Megan Bradshaw."

I smiled, taking a sip from my own glass. "You know, we could go act out the good parts of my story."

His lips curled upwards. "I thought you'd never ask."

The Debtor's Daughters

FAITHFUL BEGINNINGS

Lacey Thorn

Dedication

Chel, Chris and Carol, through thick and thin,
friends to the end.

Chapter One

Faith looked back at the house sitting on the hill behind her, the house that held all of her childhood memories and nightmares. She hated to leave her sisters behind but there was no longer any choice for her. Today was her twenty first birthday and everyone knew what that meant. Today would be her wedding day.

Her father had made it clear that since he had nothing but stupid daughters that he would get out of them what he had always wanted most. Sons or at least the equivalent. So on their twenty first birthdays they were to be wed to whatever person he had already chosen for them and become someone else's problem from that point on. But Faith couldn't do what was expected of her, was tired of even trying. So today was the day that she left this dead end town behind and faced her future on her own. The only thing she regretted was the four sisters she was forced into leaving behind.

Hope would be the oldest now, but at least at eighteen she would still have a few more years to look after the others before she was placed on the marriage block. Then there was Charity who was just sixteen and already the beauty of them all. Prudence was fourteen and all long legs and arms. And baby Destiny was just twelve and still so much a needy child that it broke Faith's heart. She had tried so hard to be the mother they had been denied. But there came a time when you either had to give in or take a stand, and Faith was ready to take a stand.

She brushed the tears from her eyes and turned back towards the woods beside the edge of the drive. No more looking back. No more dying a little more inside every day that she stayed with him. Finally it was her turn to find a life of her own as far away from Daddy and his rules as she could run. All she needed was a little faith.

She barrelled through the woods close to the road so that she could follow it as far as she could before having to veer into sight. She'd rather make her way as far as possible without being seen and returned to her father and fiancé. She shuddered at just the thought of Clifton, the man she was to marry. He was one of her dad's buddies and repulsive in every way imaginable. He was old, overweight and bald. None of which were necessarily bad but add in the fact that he had the personality of a toad and the manners of one as well and forget it. She only prayed that when the time came her sisters would fair better.

If she could get as far as the Wildlife Reserve that covered over 80,000 acres of the Texas Gulf Coast that she called home, then she might just be able to disappear completely. Or even better if she could get to someplace on the beach maybe she could slip onto a boat and just sail away. She didn't really care as long as she was gone and Daddy couldn't find her and bring her back.

Faith groaned as the first drops of rain fell and splattered on the leaves around her. Fall was known for its rainstorms and today would be no exception. If she could be sure of her position then there should be a few cabins just back in the woods. Mr. Boyd, the local banker, rented them out to different people who came to this part of Texas. Most came for the foliage and nature, but mostly for the hunting. With Thanksgiving just around the corner she hoped that there wouldn't be anyone staying there with hopes of finding a turkey.

The rain began to fall harder and she was quickly soaked through. Her white T-shirt was plastered to her chest and her well worn jeans were even tighter than they had been. She could feel the rain seeping into her shoes and soaking her socks. Every step she took through the fallen leaves had her squishing in her shoes. She thought about stopping to take her jean jacket out of her backpack, but it would just get wet as well and she might need it later if she couldn't find someplace to hide out 'til the storm blew over.

She noticed the break in the trees and was happy to see one of the cabins in front of her. It looked pretty empty from the outside, with no vehicles in sight and no smoke coming from the chimney. But she cautiously approached anyway, standing on tiptoe to glance in the window to make sure. The bed looked warm and inviting and she knew that there would be a bathroom inside with plenty of warm running water. Mr. Boyd took good care of the cabins. She stood for a moment unsure of what to do before finally heading to the door and trying the knob. It turned easily and Faith stepped in out of the rain and shut the door behind her. She turned the lock just to be on the safe side and toed out of her soggy shoes by the door before creeping further into the room.

She couldn't chance lighting a fire. That might draw someone's attention to her no matter how badly she wanted to. So she dropped her backpack by the bed and headed into the bathroom. She'd take a shower in the dark and warm up as much as she could before getting fresh, dry clothes out of her bag. If she could, she'd wait the rain out here before setting off again. She would get away. All she had to do was stay smart and alert. Her entire life was waiting for her. Anywhere but here.

* * * *

Jake Daniels stood in the shadows at the back of the cabin, partially hidden by the armoire that stood next to the office he had just finished working in. He had requested this cabin specifically for the office. He loved the way that the door blended into the wall. If you didn't know that it was there then you wouldn't even see it. He'd never been so happy about that before today.

He'd had to blink his eyes several times to make sure that he wasn't imagining the blonde haired beauty that walked into the cabin. He knew from the immediate hardening of his dick that it was none other than little Faith Coulter. He'd been coming here for years just to get a glimpse of her, which was all that her father allowed. He could understand. She was the most beautiful woman he had ever seen and Jake had seen plenty of women during his travels. But Faith was definitely one of a kind. She was a small woman, standing only five foot one or two, making her at least a foot shorter than his six foot two inch frame. But she had lush curves in all the right places, long blonde curls that swung most often in a ponytail that hung to her perfectly rounded bottom. It was her eyes that got him most. She had the biggest, deepest green eyes he had ever seen. Eyes filled with secrets, fears and, he was damn sure, passion. She was just waiting for the right man to initiate her and Jake had long ago planned to make sure that he was that man. Hell, that was why he was here now.

He had heard through his contact in town that she was to be married soon and that was one thing that he wouldn't let happen unless he knew beyond a shadow of a doubt that it was what she wanted. Then he had met her fiancé, a man old enough to be her father. The very thought of such a man touching her face, much less her body had set his gut to churning in anger. He almost laughed at the way that fate sometimes delivered what you desired most into your hands.

He had been in the office for the last few hours trying to figure out how to put a plan into motion to kidnap Faith before her wedding. Now he didn't have to. No, the woman who was constantly on his mind had delivered herself right into his hands. And if his ears didn't deceive him she was naked in the shower at this moment. He groaned and ran a hand along the rigid length of his denim covered cock. He had exactly one night to convince her that he was the man for her. One night to make sure that she was willing to leave this small town behind and explore the world with him on his boat. All he needed was a little faith. Then nothing else would ever do.

He crept stealthily on bare feet to the door of the bathroom and managed to snag her wet clothes without alerting her to his presence. He took them and her backpack into the office for safe keeping. He didn't plan on her wearing anything but him for the next few hours. He couldn't resist the impulse to raise her damp panties to his nose and inhale the scent of her sex. A groan tore from his throat though he tried hard to stifle it. She smelled sweet and hot, like warmed syrup on a cold morning. He planned to sate his hunger for her by eating that tasty pussy until she begged for him to stop. Then he would fuck her until they both screamed from the pleasure. By the time he was done with her she would be more than willing to follow him anywhere. Lord knew he already felt that way about her.

He placed the panties on the top of her pile of clothes and slipped back out of the office making sure to close the door behind him. She'd never find it, or her clothes, until he was ready for her to. The shower was still running and he smiled at how good she would look naked and dripping with water. He'd waited a long time to have his way with Faith and if he was lucky she'd have her way with him as well. If they were both lucky tonight would be only the beginning of the rest of their lives.

He moved one of the chairs from the dining table to the darkest part of the room, blocking the front door and leaving her no where to go but where he wanted her most, the bed. Any minute now his lush angel would walk out that door wondering where her clothes were. And then she'd be his.

Chapter Two

Faith reluctantly turned the shower off and reached for a towel. She was startled when all she encountered was a small washcloth. She should have paid more attention before disrobing and at least hunted for a towel. Now she was stuck trying to dry off as best she could with this tiny scrap before heading to her backpack for fresh clothes. She rubbed briskly at her wet skin, already turning cool after her hot shower.

The first thing that she noticed when she stepped out of the tub was that her clothes weren't where she had left them. The door was still open and she didn't hear any noise. No lights were on but she still felt her breath freeze in her lungs. What if someone was out there just waiting for her to step out. She was naked as the day she was born and there was nothing in the bathroom to even use for a weapon. She took a deep breath and tiptoed towards the door that led back into the main room of the cabin.

She stood there for a moment, one hand clutching the wash cloth to her chest while her other hand held the door knob behind her. If nothing else she figured that she could hide out in the bathroom, or at least try to. She peeked around the corner and didn't see anything or anyone. *Oh God!* Maybe she had left her clothes by the bed. She was so exhausted from her sleepless night and the stress she had been under recently that anything was possible.

She scurried across to the bed and searched this way and that for her backpack and clothes. They weren't there.

"Where the hell did I put them?" she murmured aloud. Then jumped and screamed when a deep voice came out of the darkness in reply.

"I moved them."

Her only covering, the minute washcloth went flying leaving her completely naked before the stranger. She turned to make a dash back for the bathroom but didn't make it more than two steps. She was swept into a pair of strong arms and pulled up against a hard chest. No matter how much she wiggled and struggled against him, he held tight. She could feel his body against hers, especially the parts that seemed to be getting harder and longer.

He groaned and Faith found herself pressed between his body and the wall, her feet dangling off the floor. His body forced her legs apart and she cried out with surprise when he ground his desire against her. He buried his head in her hair and seemed to wallow in it.

"You're better than I ever dreamed, and believe me, I've dreamed about you non stop for years now."

The voice was familiar but Faith couldn't be sure who it was without seeing his face. The only thing she was sure of was that he wasn't from around here, which could be either good or bad.

"Who are you?" she whispered. "What do you plan to do to me?"

He pulled his head back and finally she got a good look at him. She couldn't believe her eyes when she realised it was none other than Jake Daniels. It was a local joke among the women that the men wanted to drink Jack Daniels while the women just wanted a night with Jake Daniels. And Faith was just as smitten with him as every other woman in town. He had been coming here for years now and she had taken every opportunity that she could to run into him in town. He was the most gorgeous man she had ever laid eyes on. He was at least a foot taller than her five foot two inches and his black hair was long and thick hanging just past his shoulders. He had the muscled physique of a seasoned athlete. His eyes were dark as sin and his olive complexion set off his perfect smile making sure that every eye was drawn to him as soon as he entered the room.

"Jake?" she questioned. What was he doing here? And why did it seem like he was here for her?

"I wanted to woo you," he muttered burying his head in her neck, nipping and sucking at her flesh. "I wanted to say and do all the right things for you. And I will, Faith. I promise that I will. But I want you so bad. I don't think I can take it as slow and easy as I wanted to."

She moaned when he used his tongue to explore her ear and her body arched into his bringing a groan from him as well.

"Tell me you want me Faith. Tell me that you want me half as much as I want you before I die from desire." His words were a harsh rasp but she could hear the desperation in his voice. It shuddered through her as well.

She'd wanted him for years, dreamt about him being her first lover, about him sweeping her away from here and taking her with him. Maybe she couldn't have that dream but here he was offering her part of it. He could be her first lover.

"Yes," she breathed lifting her hands to clasp them in his hair. "I want you Jake."

He grasped her hips and lifted her from the wall. She wrapped her legs around his waist, keeping them aligned in all the right spots while he walked the short distance to the bed. He lowered them slowly, placing her on her back and easing down over her. It was erotic to lie naked under him while he was still fully clothed. And when he looked at her with eyes that smouldered with desire she felt moisture coat her channel in preparation for the carnal act that was soon to follow.

He groaned and eased up enough to rip his T-shirt over his head and out of the way. She was eager to explore his chest with her hands but he closed the space between them too quickly and she let them wander over his back and shoulders instead. He took her mouth with a demanding kiss, his tongue urging her to open so that he could show her what it really meant to kiss a man. It was everything that she had imagined and so much more. He tasted of peppermint and something uniquely his own and without thought she sucked greedily on him for more.

He groaned and thrust his denim covered erection against her. She cried out as the material scraped over her swollen clit, needy and ready for more, for everything. He reluctantly pulled from her lips and moved down her throat and over her chest to her turgid nipples. Her breasts were swollen and sensitive in a way they never had been before. It was like a fire in her veins when he wrapped his lips around one peak and sucked hard on her. It sent a fire deep into her belly that sent a fresh coat of moisture to glisten on her thighs and his jeans.

"I can feel how hot and wet you are," he groaned. "I knew you would be."

All she could do was moan her pleasure as he went from one nipple to the other, feeding on her as she had watched babies suckle their mothers. She could feel the tight band in her stomach grow tighter and tighter until finally it burst in a shower of stars and colours. Warmth spread through her body and a rush of fluid flowed from her.

"I want to taste you. I can feel your juices soaking my cock through my jeans." He glanced up at her and his eyes were impossibly darker, his lids heavy with desire. "I want to eat that hot little pussy until you come for me again."

She was lost in his eyes, lost in feelings that were raging through her body in a kaleidoscope. She felt like she was going to explode again from his words alone. He must have read what he needed on her face because the next thing she knew he was easing further down the bed. She felt him bury his face in the curls that crowned her sex and for the longest time he just stayed still, breathing her in like he couldn't get enough of her scent.

With a harsh sound he began to feast on her like a starving man with his first meal. His tongue played wicked torture with her lips, delving between them and running from her clit to her opening in sure strokes. She bucked and he wrapped one arm over her waist to hold her steady while using the fingers of the other hand to open her sex for his continued exploration. His tongue and teeth manipulated her clit before dipping lower. He thrust his tongue inside her and used his thumb to rub small circles around her clit. It was all she needed to send her into another wave of rippling pleasure. She ground her sex against his face, her channel milking his tongue. He stayed with her, triggering numerous tiny orgasms until she lay in a boneless heap beneath him.

Finally he pulled away from her and stood beside the bed. His face was wet from her juices but he didn't seem to mind. He reached one hand down to undo the button fly on his jeans, drawing her eyes to the bulge there. She couldn't stop the gulp of apprehension at the sight of him. And it only grew as the last button gave way and his erection sprang out, long and seeming as thick as her wrist. He seemed bigger than the ones she and Hope had glimpsed in the Playgirl magazine they had found when cleaning one of Mr. Boyd's cabins. He pushed his jeans off and stood before her as naked as she was. His fingers wrapped around his jutting cock and stroked from tip to balls while he watched her with hooded eyes.

"I'll stop if you want me to, Faith," his rough voice was at odds with his words but for some reason she believed him. "God knows that I don't want to. But if you aren't ready to take our relationship to this point yet then we'll wait."

Faith glanced at him in surprise. He spoke as if this was just the beginning of something for them instead of one night of stolen pleasure. Was he serious or just saying one of the things she had been warned that men would say to get a woman to go to bed with them? Did it really matter? She wanted him in her life. She was going to do what she wanted and damn the consequences.

"I don't want you to stop. I want you to..." She didn't know what to say. The 'F' word seemed so crude but making love was something two people did when they were going to spend the rest of their lives together. She didn't know what to say to him other than the truth. "I want you so deep inside that I can't tell where I stop and you begin."

He groaned and reached down to fumble a condom from his jeans ripping it open and rolling it on in one smooth motion. He knelt between her thighs easing them further apart. His cock nudged her opening and she automatically tensed as she anticipated the pain of her first time. But he surprised her by bending down and claiming her mouth in a soft tender kiss. It was different from their earlier kisses, sweeter and filled with promise.

Slowly she began to relax beneath him. His mouth gentled her and his hands caressed her from shoulders to thighs. She wrapped her hands around his shoulders and ran her fingers through the soft hair at his nape. He urged her to lift her legs and clasped them onto his hips and she willingly did. She felt his hand smooth over her damp curls and then the slide of his thumb over her clit.

Before long she was pumping her hips up against him desperate to feel the rub of his hard shaft along her folds. She tried to deepen the kiss but he wouldn't let her, keeping it a soft sharing instead. She cried out as he introduced a finger to her channel and thrust in and out while continuing to ply her swollen bud with his thumb. She felt the beginnings of another orgasm building within her and shuddered with anticipation. He pushed another finger into her and she exploded around him, her pussy muscles clenching around his fingers with each pulse of pleasure. He continued to push them in and out riding her through the orgasm until she lay boneless once more.

She felt his fingers withdraw first and cried out at their loss but soon realised that he only sought to replace them with something much bigger and thicker. He thrust into her with one sure move, tearing through her hymen and reaching almost to her womb. She cried out at the slight pain and discomfort but Jake held still whispering words to reassure and comfort her. She could tell by the tremble in his arms that it was costing him, but still he held himself within her, allowing her body the time it needed to adjust to his. And it was. Already she could feel her body's desire to move and she gave in to it, wiggling a little beneath him.

Jake groaned and dropped his head to her neck. "Hold still Faith. I'm hanging by a very thin thread here angel. Keep moving and its going to break."

She wiggled again as much to test him as to initiate the act itself. With a groan he slowly withdrew until only the rounded tip was still in her and just as slowly thrust back home. They both groaned at the pleasure it brought and Faith clutched his shoulders, burying her nails in his back.

"God, yes, Faith," he grunted. "Mark me as yours angel." He retreated and plunged again and then again until he had a gentle rhythm going. He nuzzled her neck and throat leaving marks of his own on her.

She wanted more, needed to feel with him what he had given her before. She wanted to feel her channel pulse with pleasure with him buried inside, needed to feel him reach his pleasure with her. "Faster," she urged canting her hips up and managing to take him deeper than before.

He granted her single request increasing his pace until he was pistoning between her thighs with a force she knew would leave her sore later. But it was worth it right now. He felt so good and the tremors were already beginning, that she now knew meant an orgasm was close.

"With you," he panted in her ear. "With you."

"What?" she struggled to ask between her own pants.

"I begin with you," he whispered. "I begin with you."

As she registered his words and what he was saying she felt the most intense orgasm so far explode in her womb and ripple out filling her limbs with heat. Her pussy tightened around him and his groan came moments before she felt him tense above her, his cock buried as far inside her as he could get it. She could feel his semen fill the condom and cursed its existence. More than anything she wanted to know what it felt like to have him and only him inside her, to have his seed fill her womb and claim her in a way that was as carnal as what they had just experienced.

"I begin with you," he murmured once more and with a contented smile Faith gave into the lethargy pulling at her, easing into sleep, secure in the arms of her lover.

Chapter Three

Jake held Faith in his arms, content to watch her sleep. He hoped that he was the reason for the smile that tugged at her lips. He would love to spend the rest of his life in just this position with her. Preferably after a night like they had just shared. God, he wanted her again. His cock was a steel rod against her thigh and it didn't help when she groaned and rubbed against it in her sleep.

He gritted his teeth but didn't even try to stop his wandering hand from exploring her naked body. She was built for love. Long, slow tender love or fast, hard fucking. She felt perfect against him, her hips and channel the perfect shelter. And her breasts were full and firm. He could suckle her nipples all day and still not get enough of her.

He dipped a finger down between her thighs and moaned hoarsely at the dew that coated his digit and her nether lips. He brought it to his mouth and sucked it clean. He loved the sweet taste of her, would gladly dine there forever. And he would do all of those things from this point on. She was his now.

He remembered the virgin's blood that had stained his cock and her thighs before he had cleaned them up earlier, while she slept content. She would never know another man the way she knew him. She had sealed both of their fates when she said that she wanted him. Now he would never let her go. He was pretty sure that she wanted the same thing but he needed to talk to her to make sure. She was the entire reason he kept coming back after that first trip. And somewhere in the years, he had fallen in love with her. Each time he saw her, learned something more about her from the townspeople, he had fallen a little deeper under her spell.

He gasped when small fingers wrapped around his cock and gave a tentative stroke along his engorged flesh. His gaze sought hers and he wasn't disappointed when he encountered the bright green eyes of Faith.

"Morning," he rasped as her hand continued to stroke and fondle.

"Morning," she whispered quietly, seeming uncertain what to do or say.

He rubbed his finger in a small circle over the bud of her clit and asked her, "How do you feel this morning? Are you sore?"

"A little," she murmured but he was happy to see that she held his gaze.

Her hand was moving faster now, her grasp more sure and firm. He groaned and thrust inside her fist before lowering his hips back to the bed. "We don't have to do anything this morning Faith. We can just talk."

She looked down at his rigid shaft and smiled up at him. "I could do the same thing for you that you did for me," she offered. And at his look of confusion she continued though a blush stained her fair checks. "Use my mouth on you."

Damn. Just the thought of her lips wrapped around his crown sucking was enough to nearly send him over the edge. Instead he rolled over on top of her and took her mouth with a slow exploration, his tongue finding and delighting in all her secret places. Finally he pulled away gazing at the moisture that stayed on her lips for a long moment before moving down her body. "You first angel."

He only skimmed over her breasts this time. More than ready to fill his mouth with her juice. His shoulders spread her legs wide and he used one hand to spread the lips of her sex so that he could fully enjoy the fragrant pink flesh inside. Her pussy was still a little red from the way they had enjoyed themselves the night before but he dipped his tongue inside to lap at the juice he saw there. His thumb moved in a circle over her clit, teasing it and making it swell bigger as her need increased.

"Ohh..." she moaned and tried to lift her hips against his face. "Yes, Jake. Yes."

He loved how eager she was, how she didn't shy away from oral sex like others might. She was new to all this and it wouldn't have surprised him if she had been more shy with her responses. But Faith was as vocal as he desired. She was not afraid to let him know how much she was enjoying what he was doing or to cry out with pleasure. Yet another reason he was falling so hard for this woman.

He used his tongue like a tiny cock, fucking in and out of her weeping slit while his mouth attached and sucked for more nectar. He pressed down with his thumb on her clit and just as he wanted she came against his mouth. He used his tongue and lips to drink her down, loving every fresh trickle of her juice. Twice more he brought her up before he eased up and used his mouth and hands to ease her down from the high.

"Make love to me Jake," she whispered when she had found her breath again. "Please."

"I don't want to hurt you Faith. You're still too tender for that," he told her even though her suggestion was what he wanted most as well.

"Just take it slow and easy with me," she suggested. "I want to feel you inside me. I need it."

God, he needed it too. He eased up her body using his tongue to caress every inch of skin along the way. Her nipples jutted out and he spent long minutes sucking and feasting on them. Finally he reached her face and bent to share her taste with her. His tongue was slow and easy and hers wrapped around it and when he slid it deeper into her mouth she sucked gently at it. She had him harder than he could ever remember being before. Harder even than the night before. He went to ease away and she grabbed him and held him fiercely.

"Don't leave me," she implored. "Not yet."

"I'm not leaving you," he assured her, squeezing her close He didn't know if she realised yet that he meant ever. "I'm just going to grab a condom off the night table there." He pointed to the box sitting opened on the table by the bed.

"Okay," she whispered and eased her tight grip on him.

He leaned away far enough to grasp a few condoms and his hips pressed firmly between hers, his cock a steel rod along her moist cunt. Faith ground her hips up against him rubbing her clit along his dick with enough force to have him fumbling.

"Easy angel," he told her and rose up to his knees between her thighs. He ripped the condom wrapper open and slid it down his shaft as quickly as he could. He gripped his cock by the base and teased it along her folds a few seconds before placing the head at her entrance and pressing forward a little.

"Watch," he told her finding her eyes with his and leading them to the place where they were slowly joining together. "Watch how your body takes me, cradles me. I love the way your pussy sucks my cock deep, the way your juices glisten all along my shaft every time I pull back. You're so tight, so hot, so fucking perfect it takes all I have to last more than a few minutes once I'm inside you."

Faith cried out as he finally impaled her sex fully with his. The cry brought his eyes back to her face and a smile tugged at his lips when he saw the blush on her cheeks. He couldn't prevent the words that tumbled from his lips, didn't even try to. "I love you Faith," he murmured then giving her no time to respond he bent and took her lips in a kiss meant to show her just how much.

He began a slow rhythm pumping his hips forward and pressing in a circular motion before pulling back out and starting again. He wanted this time to last as long as it could. He moved from her lips leaving them moist and panting as he panted his tongue along her neck and along her shoulder. He moved back up to her ear and laved and sucked at the lobe before nipping his way back down her neck.

He could feel Faith's need building, knew what she wanted by the way she rose to meet his every thrust. Still, even when she begged in her breathy whisper for him to go faster he maintained the same slow torturous pace.

"Slow and easy this time angel." It was his promise to them both. "Slow and easy."

He smoothed one hand down over her quivering stomach until he encountered her curls. He pressed his palm between them, grinding her clit with the pad of flesh just about his wrist. She responded beautifully, arching high into him taking his cock ever deeper in her tight haven. Her breath grew choppier, her eyes misted over and her hands became like talons digging into his shoulders. And he loved every moment of it.

"That's it. Come for me. Soak my cock with your cream." She cried out as much from his words he was sure as from his body's movement. Finally with a harsh cry that filled the air around them she shattered beneath him, her body sinking back into the mattress as her sheath tightened like a vice around his dick. This was what he had been waiting for.

He pumped his hips faster, every stroke taking him deep into the heart of her. He was like an animal, riding her hard and fast in his need to join her. He was amazed when he felt Faith come again, and that was all it took to send him right over the edge as well. He continued to pump inside her, small tremors that moved his cock mere inches as he felt every spurt of cum leave his dick and fill the condom. He hoped the damn thing held it all. The woman did amazing things to him. With her he was longer, thicker and she certainly had his balls full of seed. Just for her.

He dropped his weight atop her, his arms like jelly after that orgasm and unable to keep him up. He went to roll to the side and she clung to him like a vine and went with him so that they were on their sides facing one another. His cock was still semi hard inside her.

She wouldn't meet his gaze this time and he could see the tears glistening on her cheeks and lashes. He was pretty sure that he knew why but he wanted to give her the time she needed to process everything.

Finally she looked up at him. "Thank you," she whispered. "Thank you for giving me the greatest night of my life."

That sounded way to much like good bye for his peace of mind. "That was only the beginning Faith." It was a promise. To him. To her. To the world.

She surprised him with her next words. "Today's my wedding day. My birthday."

"Happy birthday," was all he could manage. Had he been wrong? Was she planning to marry the man her father had chosen? Could she possibly want to?

"Thanks," she said sadly and went to roll away from him. His cock slipped free and he knew that he should take care of the condom before it slid off and spilled on the bed sheets. But at the moment he didn't care about anything but Faith.

"Where do you think you're going?" His voice was calm and perhaps a little harder than he intended. But that was only his fear.

"I need my clothes. I have to go." She looked out at the sun that was just starting to rise outside. "I didn't make it far enough. It's too late now."

"What are you talking about?" he demanded.

She sighed and it was weary and full of sorrow. "I meant to get away last night. To just disappear and never come back. But it's too late now. They'll know I'm gone now and I won't make it far."

"Faith, look at me," he used one hand to tug her chin up so that he could see her beautiful green eyes, still dewy with her tears. "I meant what I said. I love you. I'm not letting you go. Not now, not ever. If you want to disappear then I'll help you. I'll take you anywhere you want to go. I only ask one thing in return."

Her eyes were wide pools of uncertainty and just a touch of what could be hope. "What...What do you want?"

"I want to go with you. I want to be with you for as long as you'll let me."

"Or until you grow tired of me?" she questioned and he wondered why she would ever think that would happen.

"I'll never grow tired of you Faith. I'll want you as much ten years from now as I did just a few minutes ago. You're what kept me coming back here year after year. I'd do anything just to catch a glimpse of you. I asked everyone about you, even approached your father about dating you when I learned how protective of his daughters he was."

Faith snorted at that but didn't say anything.

"I almost died when Mike called and said that you were getting married this week. I was certain that I wouldn't make it in time to stop it."

"Why?" She asked and he would swear that her heart was in her eyes.

"Because I love you Faith. I'll say it as many times as it takes for you to believe me. The thought of you with another man is torment. I want to take you away with me, marry you and when we think the time is right I want to plant my seed inside you and watch you grow round with my child."

She blushed but a smile tugged at her lips. "You'll still love me when I'm fat with pregnancy?"

He felt his heart swell with so much more than love, with everything he felt for this woman in this moment. "I'll love you every day for the rest of my life. And when you are round and glowing in the last stages of pregnancy I'll cherish every moment, every inch and every pound that shows me how much you want me and my child. I'll be your shelter, your comfort, your lover and your best friend. I'll be everything you need from this moment on. I'll love you with all I am and pray for the day when you'll love me the same."

"I do," she whispered.

"What?" he asked to afraid to hope that she might already mean that she was starting to fall for him as well.

"I do love you." Her small voice sent tendrils of warmth through him. "I used to find excuses to come into town when

I knew that you were there. I would make up errands that needed to be done just to get a glimpse of you. The women in town all joke that the men may need some Jack Daniels but all we want is a little Jake Daniels."

Jake could feel his cheeks and face warming with a blush and marvelled at what Faith could do to him. Then slowly his lips tipped up into a smile and he laughed out loud.

"What's so funny?" she smiled up at him and Jake squeezed her tight against his chest.

"Here we were doing the same things to see each other and neither of us realised it."

"Yeah, I guess you're right," Faith sighed and burrowed closer to him.

"You know what I was doing last night when you snuck in here to get warm and dry?" he asked her.

"What?" she whispered and he groaned at the feel of her tongue darting out to lick along his chest.

"Planning how I was going to kidnap you and convince you that you would be much happier sneaking off with me than staying here and marrying a man old enough to be your father."

It was her turn to laugh now. "I sort of helped you out with that one, didn't I?"

"You did," he agreed. He glanced to the window where the sun was still making its way into the day. "How soon do you think they'll come looking for you?"

She tensed beside him and glanced back to the window as well. "Soon. Dad probably already knows that I'm gone."

"Then let's get up and get dressed angel. My bike's out back and if we hurry we can be gone before anyone even knows it."

"Where are my clothes?" she asked and Jake grinned again.

"I hid them last night while you were in the shower." He jumped out of bed and went over to the hidden door that led into the office. Slipping inside he grabbed her stuff off the desk and headed back to her. "Here you go. Hurry up and get some clothes on." He was already pulling on a pair of jeans from a duffle bag that must have been under the bed. She sat up and looked down when she felt something cool against her thigh. It was the used condom from their last round of lovemaking.

"Lose something?" she inquired and grinned when he flushed again.

Jake pulled a shirt on and rounded the bed to remove the used condom from the bed but it had already spilled and left a stain on the sheets. He grabbed the opened box of condoms and placed them reverently in the duffle before pulling out a pair of socks and sitting down to tug them on. "Get going woman. We have places to go. Things to see." His eyes turned to hers and there was no missing the heat in his gaze. "Love to make."

"Again?" she whispered reaching for her fresh clothes in her backpack and hurrying to slip into them while he bent to put his shoes on.

"It's only the beginning for us Faith." There was promise in both his voice and gaze. "Only the beginning."

For Faith it was the beginning of the life she had always hoped and prayed for.

Neither the man nor the woman noticed the man who stood in the shadow of the trees watching as they loaded their few bags onto the back of the big black motorcycle. He watched as they embraced, became lost in a kiss that expressed more than passion, but the beginnings of love as well. It was all he could have ever hoped for. He was a proud man and he paid his debts but some things were more important than money. His daughters were one of them.

He was a hard man and he expected his daughters to do what he said. He didn't treat them with as much love as he should have and he was known to have a heavy hand at times. But he did love them and he refused to let his problems condemn them to a life they didn't deserve. It was his debt and eventually he would find a way to pay it.

He watched as his oldest hopped on the back of the bike and headed out of his life, probably for good. It was for the best he reminded himself, though he did nothing to wipe the tears from his checks. He had loved their mother with all his heart and just hadn't been thinking when he had made the deal after her death. The deal that had allowed him to stay on the farm and raise his daughters. It was only after it was too late that he came to his senses and realised what he had done.

But it was too late to change now. All he could do was try his best to make sure that each of his daughters escaped when the time came. After Faith's disappearance he knew that Clifton would have his men watch the girls as well. He had three years until it would be Hope's turn at the altar. Three years to make sure that everything was in place for her as well.

He might be a lot of things but only one thing was he proud of. He was a father to five of the most beautiful girls in the world. And one by one he would do what he had to in order to save them from himself.

LUST DETECTOR

Ann Cory

Dedication

Dedicated to my husband who keeps the muse
alive and well

Chapter One

Savannah Scott pulled her cherry red Ferrari over the moment she noticed the flashing lights. With her manicured fingernails, she unfastened the top two buttons of her tight knit shirt low enough to show off her lacy red push-up bra. With hurried grace, she checked her lipstick and smoothed a hand over her perfectly coifed hair. From the mirror, she gazed longingly at Officer Downs as he sidled up to her car, dressed in his fitted uniform, his powerful legs well concealed. With a deep breath she put the window down, offering a demure look.

"Afternoon, Officer."

He nodded, face devoid of any emotion. "Ms. Scott."

Goose bumps spilled along her skin at the close proximity of his cock, restrained tightly inside his pants, just beyond her door.

Reaching up, he removed his sunglasses, revealing his smouldering brown eyes. Eyes she imagined undressed her every time they had one of their confrontations. And to her delight, there'd been many.

Voice full of sweetness, she prompted him for conversation. "Pleasant day for a drive, don't you think, Officer?"

He stroked the back of his neck, and switched the weight on his foot, swinging his groin closer in her direction. The gesture alone sent a fresh batch of goose bumps along her skin.

"Yes, it is. But not above the speed limit," he added huskily. "We both know it's thirty-five miles per hour through here."

Savannah toyed with her necklace, the silver pendant circling between her breasts. "I know. I'm sorry. It's the weather. My air conditioner at home is broken, so I came out here to cool down." In a quick motion, she swept her hand across her chest and traced the neckline of her shirt, until she hit the swell of her breast.

If her eyes didn't deceive her, his bulge grew bigger.

From his shirt pocket he pulled out a pad and pen. This would be the tenth ticket she owned with his name scrawled on it. She loved everything about his signature. Strong and stately, the way she pictured him naked.

"I can appreciate your need to cool down, ma'am, but this makes the third time I've pulled you over in a week."

While her neighbours thought a woman of her age should drive something more low-key, she preferred things hard and fast. "Well, you know what they say. Third times a charm." To underscore the charm expression, she batted her eyelashes. The look on his face said he wasn't buying it, so she switched tactics. "No, you're right, Officer. I've definitely learned my lesson. You could always get me off with a warning."

His eyes widened. "Pardon me?"

Savannah feigned innocence and giggled. "I meant, let me off with a warning."

Head raised, he looked around, sighing deeply. The warm breeze rustled his black hair. Midnight black. Black as oil.

"You really need to watch your speed, ma'am. I'd hate to take your license away from you."

Bottom lip out, she nodded her head. "Oh, I understand, Officer."

Her mind raced as he tapped the paper with his pen. She could easily reach out and unzip his pants. Slip her hand inside and feel the length and width of his erection. Stroke him to a climax right then and there.

Not daring to cross the line, she turned her gaze upwards, watching the deep crease in his forehead as he pondered whether to write her a ticket or not.

"Okay, Ms. Scott, I want you to listen to me carefully. I'm going to give you the benefit of the doubt and not write you up. This time. Next time I catch you, there will be severe consequences. Understand?"

Savannah bathed in his commanding tone, almost baiting her with a hint of a challenge. Severe consequences? What could those be? Moisture between her thighs increased at the delicious thoughts. He could handcuff her. Spread her pussy wide with his baton while he tongue-fucked her clit. Search beneath her bra and panties for any concealed weapons. Or take her in the back of his squad car with her legs wrapped around his neck.

Warmth spread across her face. Already she'd forgotten what he told her.

"I'm sorry, Officer Downs. Could you repeat the last part?"

Mild annoyance crossed his youthful face. "You understand that I won't be lenient on you next time I catch you out here speeding?"

Amused at the prospect, she gave him her best come-hither look. "Yes, I do understand. If I'm naughty, you're going to punish me. Agreed."

She saw the twitch to his lips.

"Good afternoon, Ms. Scott."

"It is now, Officer Downs. Thank you."

Her body convulsed as she watched him walk away, swinging his tight ass from side to side. Savannah waited for him to drive away before she pulled back out onto the road. Headed for home, she beamed with pride.

Infatuated with younger men in uniform, she often drove around checking them out, but ever since she'd laid eyes on Officer Downs, she'd remained monogamous with her flirtations. New to the police force, he went strictly by the book and wrote her up each time he pulled her over. But she didn't care. It gave her more opportunities to spend a few moments with him, soaking in his godly physique and inhaling his musky spice scent.

Her car wasn't the only thing speeding along, so was time. Already, four weeks had passed since she'd nearly rammed into a car in the police station parking lot. From around the corner had jogged a handsome beast looking to be in his mid to late twenties, dressed in a pair of tight shorts that showed off well-defined muscles and packing some considerable size below his waist. Dazed and aroused, she'd sat back and rubbed her clit to a swift orgasm. She liked the new eye candy and badly wanted to seduce the wrapper right off him.

Later that same night she couldn't sleep. Not even chamomile tea or infomercials could sway her mind from the young man. His hard lines and toned abs were forever etched in her mind. Three orgasms later, thanks to her White Stallion vibrator, she'd come up with a plan to get his attention, and so far it was working out well.

Today was the first time he didn't write her up, and she wondered if he was warming to her not-so-subtle advances. If only he didn't call her ma'am. It made her feel her age.

Savannah pulled into her long, circular driveway and parked in front of the sunflower stepping-stones. After her divorce she'd wanted to start new. With a small trailer stuffed full of her personal belongings, she'd driven from Georgia to Oregon and settled on a charming country cottage surrounded by Douglas firs and wildflowers. Her momma had been right about putting money away every month for a rainy day, and that particular day when she left had been pouring.

Snuggle Bum, her Maine Coon cat, greeted her with a demanding mew and stretched his back high like an orange and white striped rainbow. She'd resigned herself to only one cat, not wanting to end up an old maid with a houseful of felines.

Savannah reached down and ran her fingers along the purring fur ball. "Missed me, did you? Let's get you a treat for being such a good guard kitty."

Sunshine poured into the kitchen from the skylight, heating the room like a sauna. She glanced outside at the sparkling water in her pool and considered swimming a few laps. It was about the only form of exercise she could tolerate. Fortunately her mother had blessed her with good advice and good genes.

From a ceramic bowl with kitten paw prints on the side, she grabbed a handful of salmon flavoured snacks and sprinkled them on the floor. Thirsty, Savannah poured a glass of iced tea and added a spoonful of sugar. While the cool liquid remedied her parched throat, it did little for the heat between her thighs. In her mind she'd put together a close to perfect male, and out of the blue, he'd appeared. Since then her libido had been on fire.

Close friends had warned her about dating a cop, claiming they were bad news, terrible with commitment and were married to the job. Savannah appreciated their concerns, but she was well beyond addiction. Not only did the young enforcement hottie rev up her internal engine, he'd also revved up the intensity of her fantasies. Mornings she woke covered in sweat, her clit swollen and on fire. A couple times she'd half expected to wake up and find him next to her. While her toys eased the burning need to orgasm, they did little in sating her fully.

Each fantasy seemed to compete with the last, driving her to sexual insanity. Dreams of being shackled spread eagle in a cell with bars wide enough for his cock to slide through, taking turns thrusting inside her pussy and ass. Dreams of being hogtied in his squad car, the lights flashing, siren blaring, as he stretched every orifice to full capacity, repeatedly until spent.

Savannah hoped his commanding authority came out in foreplay, too. She needed a man with the confidence to take a strong stand in the bedroom. A man who catered to her needs, cared about what she wanted, and liked to explore a little kinkiness.

For the time being, she would have to be content with their brief interludes, though they were torture. He didn't seem to mind pulling her over. Of course, he was probably humouring her and thought her some crazy woman going through early menopause or something. She liked that about him. But she longed to learn more. More than anything she longed to see him out of his uniform.

Restless, she rested her elbows on the counter and sighed. She glanced longingly towards the pool with its promise of refreshing ripples lapping at her body then towards her computer desk in the corner. Data entry work loomed, her mainstay for income, as did her list of clients for an at home cosmetics company she signed on with. None of it sparked her interest. It would all be there later.

Instead she made herself comfortable beneath the ceiling fan with her iced tea and a good book about a sexy alpha male she likened to Officer Downs.

* * * *

Alec Downs shook his head as he drove up and down the streets. He couldn't get the temptingly sweet scent of fresh peaches out of his mind. Fresh peaches and cream that is, the heavenly scent wafting from between Ms. Savannah Scott's thighs.

Damn her short skirts and tight tops. At first glance he'd have pegged her for thirty, but her driver's license claimed thirty-eight, ten years his senior. Obviously she took very good care of herself, at least from what he'd seen — and he wanted to see more. Ever since high school he'd been drawn to older women. How they dressed. Smelled. Acted. They had class, distinction and radiated a mysterious confidence. Girls his own age annoyed him, spending too much time trying to be what they thought he wanted instead of figuring out what they wanted. Savannah radiated confidence and oozed raw sexuality. It drove him mad.

He ran a hand through his hair. Fuck she loved to flirt. A temptress on wheels. Between her mesmerising powder blue eyes, ruby lips, and sun-kissed skin, he had a tough time focusing on his duties. Half the time he recited regulations that came out in a jumbled mess. She made both his job and his cock hard, as evident by his fierce erection.

Alec cranked up the air conditioner inside the patrol car. Either the humidity was getting to him or the encounter with Ms. Scott was. Her voluptuous body spiked his pulse up several notches whenever he pictured her naked, stretched across his bed, pussy glistening. A wildcat existed beneath those long lashes and severely tight clothes. With a chuckle, he thought over her comment on getting her off with a warning. It wasn't like him to give into distractions so easily, especially where women were concerned, but she had his full attention.

He'd tried several relationships in the past, but there was always something missing. Some kind of spark. He couldn't figure it out. Sex, hell, he loved sex, but he loved it more with some adventure, and playfulness thrown in. Those things turned him on. A woman who wasn't afraid to speak up and tell him exactly what she wanted, but brave enough to handle it when he obliged.

If any woman fit those qualities, it was Savannah Scott. While he didn't know if her interests were in a fling, or something more long-term, he figured they could find a way to make it work. Up until today he'd been happy to watch her from afar. He adored her spunk and the way she batted her lashes when trying to talk herself out of a ticket. Her classic explanations only gave him more of an excuse to look at her. When he stood at just the right angle, he got a fabulous eyeful of her breasts. It made him want to bury his face between them and get lost in her soft, curvaceous spirit. Her pout was to die for. Full beautiful lips flashed from coy to a smile in half a heartbeat and sent his body into orbit. He didn't even mind that she stared at him like a piece of meat.

Savannah. Her name reminded him of hot wind and wild honey. If he wasn't mistaken, she had a hint of southern in her voice, a slight seductive drawl he enjoyed listening to. 'Course, she could say anything, and he'd like it.

Her womanly body gave off the sexiest vibe. He felt it two feet from her car when he walked up. Sometimes it was so strong he had to push himself to keep going. It spoke deep to his subconscious, making him question what he would do, how far he would go, and what the boundaries were. Little comments, said under her breath or sometimes with her eyes, baited him and reeled him closer to testing those boundaries. Her body spoke to him. Asked him to touch it, kiss it, and breathe it in.

Alec's mind often drifted as she spoke. Thoughts on how beautiful her lips would look wrapped around his cock or the way her golden thighs would feel on either side of his face as he went down on her, tasting her essence. Thoughts about what it would be like taking her in her pussy and her ass.

He wondered if she liked things kinky. Wondered how she would fair with toys and chains. Maybe she liked it sweet, and he could do that too, but her demeanour suggested daring. It wasn't so much the adventure he'd been missing in other relationships. It was the spark. Flirting. Taunting. The wanting. A dull ache crept up through his belly and pulsed hard in his groin. That ache was Savannah.

Sweat slid down the sides of his face and he pulled behind a vacant building. He unzipped his pants, sighing in relief as his cock tasted freedom. There was no way he could drive around the rest of the day in his aroused state.

Alec glanced out the windows and then scrunched down in his seat. With his fist tight around his cock, he moved up and down. Savannah. He whispered her name. He imagined his cock between her lips, between her thighs. Her peach scent lingered and infused his car. He couldn't wait to lap up her juices.

He imagined her eyes pleading, lips begging for his touch. Imagined her delicate wrists bound by handcuffs, legs splayed wide, and his for the taking. He pumped his cock hard, fist tight, knowing somehow her pussy would milk the life right out of him.

He wondered how many men she'd been with. What kind of experiences held fast in her mind. Had she ever been taken in the ass? His body convulsed at the idea. He'd fuck her good and make her forget there was ever anyone before him.

He stroked his cock faster, until a jet stream of white liquid coated his belly and hand. Panting, he gazed out the window, eyes blurred, taking in the moment.

Hot as she made him, Alec tired of only seeing her writhe in his mind's eye.

The next time he pulled her over, he *would* get her off with a warning. And take her by complete and total surprise.

Chapter Two

Savannah spent the evening flipping through magazines, trying to keep her mind off Officer Downs. He didn't make it easy for her, dressing the way he did in his uniform. His shirt stretched taut across a physique she yearned to run her hands along. His pants nestled impossibly close to his skin. She couldn't deny her fierce craving to find out the size of his cock. To smooth her hands along every hot and hard inch. Taste his rich heat.

In her mind, she was his and belonged to no one else. She'd seen him pull over other women, envy barrelling through her body. How could any woman not be blown away by his good looks? Savannah didn't know if he had a girlfriend or regular lovers, but she was safe knowing he didn't have a wife, a fact she checked each time she looked at his hands.

She pictured him authoritative, even in the bedroom. A man who knew how to please and appreciated a woman with a healthy sexual appetite. A man who knew his way around talking dirty, using toys, and when need be, a firm hand across her bottom.

Savannah grabbed her White Stallion, the only thing to satisfy her tonight. Closing her eyes she imagined his body on hers, the way he'd slide his hands along her body. With the vibrator set to low, she turned it on and groaned at the beautiful agony it created. Blood swirled through her body, her thighs tense.

Her eyes watered the moment she sped up the vibrator, her clit responding, sending chills to all the corners of her body. With the vibrator tight alongside her clit, she prodded it around, circling the taut nub, imagining his fingers, his tongue, as if there were copies of him with no other purpose than to satisfy her needs.

Turning the vibrator to high, she let it do the rest of the work as she rocked her pelvis steadily, letting the vibrations steal her away into the beginnings of an orgasm. She cried out at the top of her lungs as relief flooded her.

Eyes closed, she listened to the pounding of her pulse and the short gasps of her breath. Peacefulness washed over her and helped quiet her mind.

When she next opened her eyes, amber rays of sunlight stroked her body, bathing her in its warmth. Damn the morning had come quick. Explicit dreams of her and Officer Downs had her hot and horny already. She couldn't stop thinking about his baton inside her pussy while he thrust his cock inside her ass. It had felt so damn real. One day she hoped it would be.

Anxious for another run-in with her favourite law enforcement hunk, she hurried into the bathroom to start her day. Her hardened nipples ached as the water teased her, like a tongue. Savannah knew an orgasm was mere seconds away. Her body was already on high alert from the salacious fantasy lingering in her mind.

Showerhead in hand, she widened her stance and let the fast jets of water beat along her sensitive and swollen clit. A swift climax barrelled through her, giving her enough liberation to get her through most of the day. She smiled and worked shampoo into her hair. If only Officer Downs knew the things he did to her.

Showered and smelling of peaches, she chose a short, flowing black skirt that hit an inch above her knees and a powder blue top that hugged her with snaps running down the front. Conveniently she unsnapped the top four buttons, hitting dangerously low to her bra. In the mirror she admired her face. Minor wrinkles bracketed her eyes when she smiled, along with a few around her lips, but otherwise she hardly looked her age, or so she hoped. Still toned from years of dance, yoga, and the occasional swim, she couldn't complain. It was a long shot to think she could score with a younger man, but she could still dream.

She brushed out her long, raven hair and piled most of it on top of her head with clips, than let the rest spill around her head, little curled tendrils in front of and behind her ears.

Savannah looked over her appearance one more time and slipped on a pair of black pumps. Curious to find out what the severe consequences would be for speeding again, she got in her car and drove to her usual spot. When she caught a glimpse of Officer Down's patrol car, she pushed down on the accelerator.

* * * *

Alec couldn't help but smile as he watched the red Ferrari burst onto the scene. Turning on his lights he followed her a short distance until she pulled over. He took a moment and sat in his car. Would his plan work? The impish vixen did this to him on purpose. He knew it. There couldn't be any other explanation. But he had to find out for sure. Had to know what her true intentions were with him. It was getting to the point that he couldn't think straight because he had her on his mind...the suggestive way her breasts peeked out of her too-tight tops...the flash of skin from the slit of her skirts that always revealed more when she reached for her driver's license.

He couldn't think about anyone else except her all night long. If he didn't have her soon, he'd explode.

Alec opened the car door and bit the sides of his cheeks. He'd have to play it tough.

"Well, well, well. If it isn't Ms. Scott."

She looked up at him and her blue eyes sparkled in the sunlight.

"I'm dreadfully sorry, Officer."

Her desirable snicker wrapped around his cock and gave it a tug. This wouldn't be easy.

Clearing his throat, he tried again. "I'm afraid that the last warning was your final chance. Now, if you'd be so kind as to follow me to the police station, we'll get this taken care of once and for all."

In less than a second her suggestive smile vanished. "But...I..."

He raised his hand and shook his head. "I uphold the laws of the road, ma'am, and I feel you've taken advantage of my kindness. Either you follow me to the station, or I'll escort you there myself."

Alec bit his cheeks so hard he could almost taste blood. For once, her innocent look seemed genuine. She might have called the shots in the beginning, but things were different now.

Her lower lip quivered. "If you say so, Officer."

"I do. You're a danger out here to yourself and the other drivers. I've let you get away with things far too long."

He gazed down at her womanly breasts, embraced provocatively inside her bra. Simply breathtaking.

"Don't try anything funny, either. I'll be watching you from the rear-view mirror."

Brows furrowed, she shook her head. "I won't try anything funny."

Her breathy voice aroused him. Spoke to every part of his body. Burned away inside his groin, making his cock twitch.

Alec hurried to his car before he gave himself away then led them to the police station. What she must be thinking? He couldn't worry if he'd come on too strong. Things were about to turn interesting. Thanks to calling in a few favours from his buddies, he had the stage set for one hell of a seduction. One room, complete privacy, and a wild imagination.

In the parking lot, he signalled to a parking spot while he drove into his designated one. While she parked, he got back into character. Ready for the next part of his plan, he headed towards her and threw open her door.

"Out you go, ma'am."

She gazed at him, her thick lashes blinking slowly. "Where are we going?"

With gentle force he wrapped his hand around her arm, just above the elbow. "Inside the station."

Being so close to her peaked his arousal, making it painfully stiff.

"Do I need to fill out paperwork?"

Alec clenched his jaw, doing his best to act irritated. "No, not at this time."

Again she blinked, her eyes wide, framed with black lashes. "Am I in big trouble, Officer Downs?"

The woman deserved the truth, and he'd give it to her. "Yes, Ms. Scott. I'm afraid you've gotten yourself into a bind."

Chapter Three

Savannah didn't know what to expect. She never imagined Officer Downs would go so far as to bring her to the station. Never in a million years. Somehow her game had gotten out of hand, but still she wasn't afraid. The way he spoke to her, his voice full of authority, turned her on. Like he'd put her under some sort of spell. Warmth from his hand on her arm penetrated her body, sending sizzling jolts down to her toes. Willingly she followed, though it felt more like she floated.

He led her swiftly through the busy police station. All around her the place buzzed. Phones rang. Voices rose to loud volumes. Paper scratched through a large copy machine. They moved through the station so fast it blurred before her eyes. She did her best to stay in step with him, not too far forward or too far behind, but right at his side. Had she blown her chance with him already?

"Right in here." He led her into a small room with one very high window. Sunlight filtered in and streaked across a wooden chair with a strange looking device next to it.

Releasing her arm, he gestured towards the chair. "If you'll take a seat, we'll get right to it."

She walked to the chair, wringing her hands. "Um, okay."

His take-charge attitude made her knees buckle. She glanced around the plain white walls, empty of décor except for one large mirror. Savannah took a seat and wondered if people watched from the other side of the mirror, like they did on TV. Other than a minor fender bender at twenty-one, she'd never been on the wrong side of the law before.

Her pulse sped up as he closed and locked the door. Maybe she really had gone too far. Not sure what to expect, her gaze moved to the mirror and then back towards the door. Why had he locked it?

A charming smile bowed his lips, putting her a little at ease. "All right, Ms. Scott, first, I'm going to conduct a little test. Nothing to worry your pretty head about."

She returned her attention to Alec, as he moved the odd-looking machine closer to her.

Her mouth went dry. "Test?"

From his belt he removed a pair of handcuffs. Savannah's eyes widened. They were so strong and shiny looking. Every fantasy she'd had came crashing into her mind. She wanted those naughty things wrapped around her wrists.

His voice deepened with a whiskey-roughness. "Yes, a test, just to make sure we're on the same page. I promise not to make it too gruelling, though some of it will depend on you."

Her breath hitched at his words. Could this really be happening, or was she suffering from heatstroke? Her mind fogged as he bent down and tightened one cuff around her right wrist and the other around the machine.

"Do you know what this device does?"

Savannah looked the strange contraption over. With his close proximity she couldn't think straight. "No, I'm afraid I don't."

"It's a lie detector test. We're going to use it on you today."

She frowned. "I'm not understanding. Did I do something wrong?"

A slow, sexy smile curved his lips. "Yes, you were naughty. You've been very naughty, and it's time to get to the bottom of it."

Savannah tried to still her trembling legs.

"I'm going to ask you a series of questions, and you need to be completely honest."

"What happens if I don't tell the truth?"

"The machine will let me know. None of it hurts, I promise." He stared at her and wetted his lips. "I'd never hurt you."

His lust-filled gaze drew the moisture between her thighs, dampening her panties. She believed his words.

"I trust you Officer Downs."

He leaned over her and brought his lips up to the side of her cheek. His breath caressed her ear as he spoke. "From here on out, you can call me Alec. It will make things a little more comfortable."

An ache, deep and intense, throbbed at her core as she whispered his name, "Alec."

"I'm going to place a few of these suction cups on you. They are attached to wires from the machine, so that when you answer the questions, it gives a correct read out."

Soft pads pressed against her forehead and one around her finger. Her body tingled wherever his hands touched.

When he pulled back, his gaze drifted over her. In that moment she willingly gave him total control over her.

"Are you ready?"

After clearing her throat several times, she finally found her voice. "Yes."

"Good girl. Let's start with a few easy questions before we make our way to harder ones."

Her gaze instantly moved to his groin as he mentioned harder. She didn't know what he planned to ask, but if it had anything to do with how badly she wanted him, then she really was in trouble.

"Is your name Savannah Melody Scott?"

The way he said her name made her body convulse. "Yes, it is."

"Were you married once?"

"Unfortunately, yes."

She didn't want to think about the stupidity of her youth, or how out of spite she'd married a guy to get back at her parents. Those were five years she couldn't get back. Five years of misery.

"Would you rather I didn't ask more questions about your marriage?"

"Yes."

"Very well. I don't want to upset you. Let's see, something more basic. Do you have blue eyes?"

She swallowed hard under his tantalising gaze. "Yes, I do."

"Have you been watching me jog in the mornings?"

Savannah's face burned. She wanted to lie, but knew better. Maybe the machine wasn't such a good idea after all. Her forehead beaded with sweat. "Yes, I have."

"Have you been speeding on purpose, so that I will pull you over?"

Oh god, he'd figured it all out. The leg of his pants brushed against her skin and sent jolts of electricity throughout her body, flustering her. "Um, I—yes."

His sexy little smirk returned. "I see. So you've been breaking the law on purpose. You're a very naughty woman, aren't you?"

She didn't know what to say, afraid how the machine would interpret her words.

"One moment and I'll be right back with you." He went to the corner of the room and opened a small cooler, pulling out a tray of ice cubes. "I apologise for the stifling heat in here. I've got something to help cool us off."

Alec returned and knelt in front of her, resting a firm hand on her knee.

"Spread your legs, please."

The room instantly turned up another twenty degrees. Had she heard him right? Savannah parted her thighs, and her breath left in a rush. He was close, impossibly close.

"You're doing wonderful, by the way. So far you're passing with flying colours."

Screw the test. Could he smell her? The burning need and desire for him?

"Whenever I pull you over, I can't help but notice your beautiful breasts. The way your tops accentuate their fullness. Almost begging me to bury my face between them. Do you want me to touch them?"

A wave of heat fanned around her face. She tried to speak but only managed a gasp. Even without the handcuffs he had her pinned with his commanding gaze.

"Do you? Do you want my tongue to swirl along your nipples and suck hard until you come?"

Savannah squirmed. She wanted to scream "oh god yes", but she couldn't make her lips move.

His eyes sparkled as he smiled. "I'll take that as a yes."

Alec stood over her, his legs between hers, and unsnapped her shirt in a slow, languid motion. Her nipples hardened under his hot-blooded gaze. She wished he'd rip it the hell off instead of drawing out the torture. Each snap reverberated around the room, making her panties drenched. Savannah wondered if there was a big fat stain on the chair. She wouldn't doubt it.

How could she sit here and take this? Yes, she wanted him and had wanted him ever since she laid eyes on him. But he was going about it in a way that would truly kill her. Unless this was her punishment. A sweet hell she'd never forget.

Again he brought his lips to her ear, speaking soft and slow. "Anytime you aren't comfortable with something about this...test, you tell me. Okay?"

Savannah nodded her head. She didn't want him to stop. Her clit throbbed and she needed something, anything to stick between her legs and grind on. She'd been so used to her toys and a quick-to-satisfy mentality that the whole foreplay thing had gone right out the window.

With her shirt undone, he worked at the front clasp of her bra. Relief spread over her as the restrictive garment fell open as well, leaving her exposed.

His brows arched high. "Mm. There, that's much better. They're even more beautiful than I'd imagined. I've never felt so strongly about a woman before, and you are just that, every bit a woman."

Under his intent gaze, she flooded wet.

He reached over and took an ice cube out of the tray. "How about a little something to help cool you down?"

She could barely speak, her lips were trembling and shaky. "Yes, please."

The ice looked like shiny glass as he brought it to her skin, the sunlight reflecting right through it. In slow, gentle circles, Alec moved the ice cube along her collarbone and neck. Water trickled between her breasts and slid down to the waistband of her skirt. The refreshing trail sent a thrill fluttering through her belly.

"Have you been speeding to get my attention?"

She wanted to squeeze her thighs shut, but his thick, muscular legs were in the way. Her panties dampened more.

"Yes."

He moved the ice cube around her breasts and then circled around her nipples.

"Have you thought about me in your dreams?"

Her thighs quivered from the delicious liquid making her nipples achingly stiff.

"Yes, I have. Every night."

Alec removed the ice and leaned forward, swirling his tongue around her drenched nubs. One and then the other. She almost lost it when he bit and suckled her nipple. Her mind raced. His attentiveness floored her. Left her breathless.

He paused and in a deep, hypnotic voice asked, "Have you ever gotten yourself off? Rubbed your clit raw until you screamed? Cried out my name as you orgasmed?"

The room spun. His words sent goose bumps along her arms, but not from any kind of chill. "Yes, yes, and yes to all of those," she moaned.

Savannah hoped that if she passed this test, he would put her out of her misery.

Straightening back up he pinched both her nipples between his fingertips. His cock excruciatingly close. She felt like a rabid dog, foaming at the mouth, wanting to snap her lips over his young male hardness and taunt him for awhile. She'd deep throat him and send him through the roof.

Head tilted back, she glanced upwards to his lips, glistening wet from the melted ice he'd swirled around her nipples. The pleasure those lips gave her, almost too much, but she craved more. If only he'd kiss her.

"Do you like that I've handcuffed you?"

She goddamn loved it. "Yes."

His fingers pinched harder. "Does it make you feel dirty?"

How did he know? She nodded and sucked in her breath.

"I want to know how dirty you are."

Alec knelt down and pushed her skirt up. Her body jerked in response. Impossibly close. How could she take this much longer?

A lustful glance spread across his face. "Mm, I can smell how badly you want me. I'll bet you like an authoritative partner in the bedroom. A lover who knows your needs by the sound of your breath. A lover who can't wait to explore you and satisfy every single need."

He knew her all too well. Body trembling, she watched him hook his thumbs beneath the sides of her panties. Savannah raised her hips slightly as he slid them down. She could only imagine how wet they were. Stained with her juices.

He took a whiff and dropped them to the floor. "I have a confession to make since you've been honest with me. I've wanted you since the first day I pulled you over. Did you know that?"

She shook her head.

"It's true. You've no idea how relieved I was to learn you were divorced. I only hoped you were single."

A tear played at the corner of her eye. "Me too. I mean, I hoped you were single."

He splayed her thighs further apart. Her body burned from his touch. "I've enjoyed our little intrigues. And I knew what you were doing, or at least I thought I did, but I wanted to be sure. I hope our age difference doesn't bother you."

Here she'd worried the same thing. Nearing forty she hadn't thought this could ever happen for her. She noticed the crease along his forehead deepened. Shocked, she hadn't expected him to feel insecure.

"No, it doesn't."

The crease on his forehead disappeared as the corner of his eyes crinkled up. "Good. Do you know what turned me on most about you?"

Savannah stared deep into his eyes. "No."

"Your confidence. It's intoxicating. Now everything about you turns me on."

His palm cupped the heated flesh between her thighs.

"If you want me to stop, you just say the word."

She wanted to say he was in no danger of that, but her throat filled with imaginary cotton, making it difficult to string any words together.

"Otherwise, I'll keep going."

Taking another ice cube from the tray he teased her clit with it. She swallowed back a cry. Head lowered, he swept his tongue along the same trail as the ice. Savannah groaned at the cool contact. She tried to grab his head and vaguely remembered her one wrist cuffed to the machine. With her other hand she raked her fingers along his silky hair.

"You taste wonderful. Peaches and cream."

He circled her clit again with his tongue. Her vision blurred, unable to focus on anything. She almost hoped people watched from behind the mirror. Watched how a woman should be touched. Watched her get the fuck of a lifetime. Every stroke of his tongue zapped her with electric heat. If only he'd give her a little taste of freedom, a small slip of his fingers between her wet folds to further awaken the carnal beast inside.

As if he read her mind, Alec thrust two fingers inside her, relentless in his speed. God, he was going to bring her to the brink any minute.

"You're unbelievably wet and so damn tight."

She wanted him to find out just how tight with his hard length as she wrapped her legs around his waist and wait for his cock to jet into her.

Her blood swirled beneath her skin as his fingers ignited an inferno in her belly. Waves of lush pleasure lapped at her scorching centre. She rocked her pelvis forward, squeezing her thighs tight on either side of the chair. His hair against her inner thighs only amplified her need to come. Another two fingers entered her and increased the friction as he suckled her clit.

Between his masterful tongue and deep plunges, she couldn't breathe, couldn't grasp air. Her pulse drummed in a swift cadence, the beat drowning all sound out, until her orgasm slammed through her body and her voice escalated to a full, Banshee cry. Several spasms drove through her as he removed his fingers and kissed her belly.

"You taste so damn sweet."

She blinked back the glaze and watched him rise to his feet. His eyes stole over her possessively.

"Now for another question, and remember, don't lie. The machine will tell me if you do."

So far she couldn't lie, even if she wanted to. Everything he'd asked her had been nothing but the truth. In a mad flash he took off his shirt. His thick, sculpted muscles bulged in all the right places. Everything tight and toned. A firm terrain she wanted to explore with her hands, lips, and tongue.

He unzipped his pants and slid them down along with his black briefs. His fingers stroked his thick flesh.

"Tell me, is this what you want?"

Savannah gasped at the sight of him fully erect. "Oh god, yes."

* * * *

Alec bent down and ran his hand up over her black heels, along the curve of her calves, admiring the beauty and softness of her skin. The shapeliness of her legs caused his balls to tighten. He loved legs, womanly legs, with healthy thighs. Her scent—hypnotic, making him want to thrust his cock into her without hesitation, but part of this scenario was to play it out, and make her go crazy waiting.

He leaned over and cupped her chin, tilting her gaze towards him. The passionate heat in her eyes penetrated his skin.

His lips captured hers and he pressed tight. She all but fell into him. An obvious hunger existed between them as their tongues tangled, turning deep and primal. He almost couldn't get enough. The intensity of their kiss left him winded, but so damn hungry for more. To take her, fuck her, make her shudder. As the kisses turned rough, her hand reached out and stroked his cock, almost making him come right there. If she did that again he'd lose it entirely. He needed to take back control.

Alec pulled away and gave her a severe look.

"Let's get back to my line of questioning, shall we? I said I'd punish you the next time I caught you speeding, and still you ignored the limit. Did you forget?"

She gave him a coy look. "No, that's why I did it."

Surprised by her sheer honesty, he almost faltered. "I see, so you took it as a challenge rather than a warning?"

A fire blazed behind her eyes. Dark with heat. A strong hunger for more of what he could and would give her.

"How else could I take it? I get so hot for you that my mind just hears what it wants. I wish I could say I'm sorry and that

I'll never do it again, but with you out there, I don't know, something just comes over me."

Her voice dripped with an animalistic need. Alec couldn't hold back much longer. He needed to be inside her. Fuck her hard like she wanted.

"Do you like being told what to do during sex?"

She stared at him hard, her face flush. "Yes."

"Good. Then I want you to stand, turn around, and place your hands on the chair."

Without hesitation she obeyed, the handcuff twisting as she turned. He pulled her skirt all the way off, not wanting anything to come between them.

His gut tightened. On her lower back he noticed a beautiful rose tattoo, crimson red. One more thing to turn him on.

"You're stunning." Alec admired her luscious hips, ass, and deep pink slit. "I love the way your juices glisten against the sunlight."

"Is anyone watching?"

His brow crinkled briefly. "Ah, the mirror. No, it's not a two-way mirror and there aren't video cameras set up in here. I promise, the only one looking at you is me."

He ran his fingers between her thighs and fondled her clit. Instantly she pressed back into him.

"I can't wait to have you in private, all of you with your full naked body bent over my bed. My lips kissing the curves of your womanly form. I can't wait to restrain you with ropes and cuffs, suspend you in the air in a swing with my cock driving in and out of your hot pussy."

Her groans escalated in volume, legs shaking violently. In torturing her, he only tortured himself.

Savannah looked over her shoulder, eyes pleading. "Please, don't make me wait."

To prove her need, she held her ass up high, proud. With his legs he helped spread her thighs wider.

"Do you want me, Savannah? Do you want me to shove my cock up inside you? Stretch you like no other lover can?"

Her body bucked at his words. Without waiting for an answer, he pressed into her slick pussy.

Alec shuddered at the collision of his cock inside her liquid heat. Loved the way he felt inside her, and how she clenched her inner muscles tight around his shaft. He couldn't get enough of her, she hit every one of his nerve endings and let it race around him. His pulse pounded as he thrust in and out, watching the way her juices coated his length. He focused on her red rose tattoo. Imagined it turned a darker shade of red the closer she came to an orgasm. All the while her voice rose in octaves from grunts to full out bellows.

Hands around her hips, he pushed in deeper, pumping harder. Her sounds spurring him on. He wanted, needed more. She was letting him get too hot too fast.

Slowly he slid out from her and played with her clit as he reached for his pants.

"Have you ever had it up the ass before, Ms. Scott?"

She glanced back at him, eyes twinkling. "Yes, once."

"Did you like it?"

"Very much."

"I'll bet you did. One second here, I have something you'll appreciate."

From his pocket he pulled out a tube of lubrication. He spread the cool gel all around her puckered hole. Carefully, he slid two fingers inside, and then three, stretching her, readying her. His pulse throbbed in his cock, begging for what was about to come. With ease, he spread her bottom.

"I'm going to shove my cock far up inside you, do you understand?"

Her breathy moans were answer enough.

"Then I'm going to rub your clit so fast, I expect you to come twice."

Alec swiftly rolled on a condom and pushed his cock through her little sphincter hole. He nearly reeled at the immediate sensation. Tight and packed with heat. It was like a goddamn chokehold around his dick and he went to town on her. He bit his lip to keep from shouting loudly. It wouldn't take much more and he'd be coming hard.

The shortness of her breath let him know she was close, too. He pumped hard, grazing his fingers along her swollen clit, rubbing faster and faster until he felt her whole body buck beneath him. She cried out and he thrust faster, harder, going as deep as he could possibly manage, his balls slapping against her.

"You're so tight, unbelievably tight."

Savannah moaned, her body trembling fiercely.

"Oh god, another one. I'm going to come again," she cried.

Again he massaged her clit, pumping away inside her, gearing her up for an amazing climax. The second time she cried out, he thrust into her and pulled out. Nothing prepared him for the extreme high he experienced as spasms overwhelmed him. He could hardly see straight. Sweat streaked down his face and along his chest.

Spent, he moved on shaky legs to grab a towel from the cupboard to clean her off and disposed of the condom. Alec pulled the suction cups off and removed the handcuffs. Gingerly he gathered her in his arms. He loved the feel of her breasts heaving against his chest.

She fixed her eyes on him, her lips swollen from their feral kisses. Twisting a strand of hair around her finger, she asked, "I take it you're done with your questions?"

The woman was amazing. Unbelievably phenomenal. He could spend a lifetime finding new ways to make her scream.

"Nope. I have a few more. Completely harmless, I swear."

Savannah gave him an adorably puzzled look.

"What about the machine?"

He flashed a sheepish grin. "I never even turned it on."

Chapter Four

Savannah pulled back from his embrace, but not very far. "What?"

He shrugged. "It doesn't even work, as far as I know. All I had to do was convince you it worked."

Her bottom lip puffed out. "You tricked me."

He kissed her lip and laughed. "I guess I did. It was more of a lust detector than a lie detector. Tell me you didn't enjoy yourself."

Even with the knowledge she could lie if she wanted, Savannah spoke the truth. "Well, I can't."

"And tell me you didn't have your own agenda speeding in your car while I was on duty."

There wasn't a thing she could say back to that. "Guilty."

Alec sat on the chair and patted his thighs. "Have a seat on me."

Her body ached to feel his warmth again. "With pleasure."

His heart thudded against her body as she climbed on him, sitting sideways.

He traced his finger around her jaw line and tapped her nose. "So, do you think you can like me for more than just my fit body and good looks?"

She laughed so hard tears welled in her eyes. "Of course. I mean, I won't pretend that you weren't lust at first sight, because you were. But I guess you do have other qualities, too. The way you carry yourself. How you enforce the law." She winked and he broke out into laughter.

"Yes, well, trust me when I say no one else will ever get that kind of interrogation from me again."

Savannah smiled. "I'm glad to hear you say so. I wouldn't want to think you treat all the ladies who speed that way. I kind of hoped I was special."

He nodded. "You are. 'Course, I may not be the guy you're looking for." His fingers traced up and down her arm, sending delicious shivers over her skin. "I'm sure you've heard life with a cop can be unsatisfying."

"If what we just did is any kind of indication of that being true, then I'm all for it."

He puffed out his chest and sucked in his cheeks. "You just like me for my uniform. I knew it. I should have kept you hooked up to the machine."

She snuggled in closer to him, enjoying the feel of his chest, damp with sweat. The room was infused with the scent of their sex.

"Well, there is the uniform thing. And your young, tight, hot body. Your face isn't entirely painful to look at either."

"I appreciate you saying so."

Savannah snorted. "I'm curious. Whatever made you decide to become a cop?"

"Believe it or not, I actually planned to be a teacher. You know, save one student at a time. Find a way to keep kids in school and have fun doing it. But, another opportunity presented itself to me and I felt obligated to take it."

She caught the seriousness of his tone and didn't know whether to press him further or not. "Is it too personal to talk about? Because if it is, I'll understand."

"I grew up in a rough neighbourhood in downtown Portland. My dad split when my baby brother was born. I was about five at the time. Guess he wasn't mature enough to handle two kids. Couldn't keep a job. Refused to stay sober long enough to clean up his act. Wasn't ever there anyway. My mom ended up working two jobs and taking evening classes just so we'd have a roof over our heads and food on the table. She raised us the best way she could and I've never forgotten that. Promised we'd have a better life one day."

"Sounds like you have a great mom."

"Yes, we're still very close. After she graduated from night school, she received a job offer to come work for a company in Corvallis. Two weeks before we were going to move, my brother got shot. It wasn't an accident, either. Guess he witnessed some activity he shouldn't and threatened to go to the police about it. My brother thought he was a superhero. He was only eleven."

She cupped his cheek and kissed the crease of his forehead. "I'm so sorry, Alec."

"Thanks. He had such a good heart."

"Did the ones who killed him ever get caught?"

"Eventually. The case got tied up in court for several years. Witnesses wouldn't talk out of fear. Stories kept changing. The bad guys held all the power. I sat there, my mom crying her eyes out, begging for some justice, and the whole thing made me sick."

Savannah hated that he'd gone through such a horrific tragedy. "But they did get caught, right?"

"Yeah. And every time they come up for parole, my mom and I are in there to make sure they remain locked up. The justice system is far from good, but I try and hold onto the fact that I'm fighting the good fight. I mean, I can't change everything, but the least I can do is try. Uphold the law, punish the bad guys, serve and protect. I do it as a way to honour my brother."

"You're a very noble and brave man. I'm sure he appreciates it. He'd be proud of you."

"I think so too. Well, now that you know why I became a cop, I want to know why you're into cops."

"Cop. Singular. I'm only into one cop."

"Damn straight. But, you know, dating a cop comes with a whole bunch of complications."

"Why, because you put your life on the line? I think it's amazing that there are people out there doing what you do. Out there risking their lives. Saving lives. Being real heroes. Getting all sweaty and looking mighty fine doing it."

He laughed. "So, you're okay with it?"

"I'm very supportive of it. I wish I had the courage to take those kinds of risks. I'd be proud to know my man is out there doing good. Damn proud."

"You're just saying that because I handled you well. Admit it."

"I never imagined I'd be interrogated in such a rewarding way. You handled me like no other man ever has."

"I'm not sure I want other men handling you."

"Good."

"I think I'd like to see you exclusively, Ms. Scott. Preferably when I'm off duty."

Savannah nuzzled her nose against his and kissed his cheek. "Enough with that Ms. and ma'am stuff. I'm your woman. Got it?"

"Got it."

"Are you off duty now?"

"Well, technically my shift is over, but —"

She reached down and stroked his cock, admiring the way it sprang to life effortlessly.

"Mm, then I think I need to shift over."

Savannah turned so her back faced him. Reaching between her legs, she guided him into her as she sat back into his lap, her legs over his. The plunge was explicit and nearly knocked the wind out of her. She felt every inch push inside her, stretching her inner walls to full capacity. Her body shook with each unhurried thrust and grind. A single tear rolled down the side of her face, she wanted to savour this moment. He kneaded her breasts in his hands, rolling her nipples between his fingers.

Blood raced through her veins in a frenzied panic, her heart pounding in a quick drumbeat cadence. All the energy united to her core, circling like a whirlpool, just waiting for the right moment to break free. She rolled her hips, sliding up and down his big cock, shivering each time he splayed her further apart. Grinding into him like she was a never-ending vessel, unable to reach a point of too far.

"You're killing me, woman," he whispered, his lips tenderly brushing her earlobe.

He moaned and sighed into her neck, pinching her nipples tight.

"Just wait until I put cool metal clamps on these babies, then you'll really scream."

To prove his point, he pinched harder. The powerful sensation rocketed through her. She clenched her pussy tight around him, riding his cock fiercely. Tightening down on him, milking him. She was relentless in her desire to bring him to a strong climax. At the same time he slid his hand between her thighs and circled her clit.

"I want to feel you come all over my cock. Come for me."

Savannah leaned her head back against him, almost whining as he manipulated her clit into complete submission with one hand, the other still pinching her nipple. Locked in a manic rhythm, she came down on him, repeatedly, riding his length, burying him deep in her moist heat.

He suckled at her neck and the blood swirled inside her head. Nothing else existed in the moment except their bodies, rabid with heat, savagely racing towards an orgasm to send them out of this world.

"Faster, rub my clit faster," she moaned, her head moving side to side.

A plethora of vibrations resonated in her body, blazing a scorching path that seemed endless. She cried out as the orgasm shot through her, ripping through her like nothing she'd ever felt before. Complete satisfaction filling ever ounce of her being.

His whispered words kept her floating in the euphoric high. "I love the way your pussy contracts around my cock."

The slow burn in her thighs lessened. She wasn't through with him yet, and she had a plan of her own. Quickly she stood and turned.

Savannah knelt between his legs and wrapped her hand around his hard, pulsing cock. She stroked it. Enjoyed the texture. Loved the way it spasmed in her palm. How it smelled of her sex. His husky groans said enough to her, it was what he wanted as well.

Alec reached over and rustled her hair. "What do you think you're doing, woman?"

She batted her eyelashes. "I want to watch you come."

"Haven't you had enough?"

Lips pursed, she chuckled. "You should know by now that I'm a persistent woman."

His brown eyes smouldered. "Yes, in a way that drives me wild."

Wanting to taste him, she flickered her tongue along his cock. Before he had a chance to react, she grabbed the handcuffs and chained him to the machine, as he'd done to her. She kind of liked the role reversal.

Eyes narrowed, he gave her a look of reprimand. "Savannah, you're getting yourself into trouble again."

With a coy smile, she rolled her tongue along the underside of his cock, her gaze trained on his. In delight, she watched his face flush as her lips enveloped the tip of his head, and took his entire length inside her mouth. He shook as she skimmed her lips back and forth along his shaft, sucking intensely. Her fingers teased at his balls, lightly prodding them while she worked her mouth, lips, and tongue. It was her turn to take him over the edge.

She ran her tongue along the underside of his cock again and watched his muscles tense. His fingers tangled in her hair.

"You shouldn't. Please, Savannah. I don't think I can take it. Come sit on my lap again."

She slipped her mouth off and stroked his cock firmly in her fist. It gave her such a rush to be the one in control now. Sweet as she could, she gave it to him straight.

"Officer Downs. Consider yourself warned. This time I plan to get you off."

HOT AND HUMID

Shermaine Williams

Dedication

For Samantha, a wonderful sister,
with love and gratitude.

Chapter One

"Jeanette…Jeanette, de bus comin'," my aunt called with an unnecessary sense of urgency.

I had heard the music playing but ignored it on the basis that music was always playing and anyway, I was busy getting ready. Taking another quick look at myself in the mirror, I wondered whether it was wise to wear shorts, but it was too late now. Besides, the shorts were quite long and baggy and served to cover my ample backside – known as 'The Bubble' – pretty well.

Despite the music blaring from the speakers, the driver still felt the need to announce his presence by beeping the horn, which didn't please Aunt Yvonne.

When I had called her to ask if I could come and stay, she made it seem like I was being ridiculous by even asking. She was happy to accommodate me on my whim.

In order to briefly escape from the rut that was my life, I'd decided to take a spontaneous holiday in my parents' native Grenada, determined to have as much fun as possible before returning to my life of work, bills, cold weather, useless men and general malaise. A life that was just too damn boring for words.

Once I'd made the decision to go away, there was no question that I would opt for anywhere other than The Isle of Spice. I'd been several times before, though not for a few years, and just felt comfortable. It was like coming home. Sometimes I liked to imagine what my life would have been like if I was born here, if I emigrated even, but alas, it was merely a pipe dream. I have a mortgage to concern myself with now.

Grabbing my rucksack, I hurried out of the bedroom in time to hear my aunt complaining about the apparent impertinent gesture.

"Wha' da damn man blowin' for?"

I could only smile, knowing that as cantankerous as she seemed, she was a lovely woman. She had organised this day out for me. Usually when I'm in Grenada my time is spent either visiting family and friends or lying on the beach. But when I told her that I wanted to enjoy myself and blow off some steam, she told me about a man she knew who might be able to help in that regard.

He worked at one of the hotels in St. Georges and organised the excursions for 'de rich people an' dem'. Although I wasn't staying at the hotel, he agreed to get the mini-bus to stop off and pick me up for a day of hiking in the mountains. Now I'm not the fittest person in the world, but even if I was, who in their right mind goes hiking in this heat? And that's coming from a sun worshipper!

But Aunt Yvonne was still enthusiastic on my behalf, saying it would be nice for me to see some parts of the island that I hadn't seen before. It was a good point, so I tried to put my apprehensions aside and enjoy it. Besides, I could probably do with getting in shape—my figure wasn't exactly attracting any fine specimens—and what better way to start than to go for a hike? With a quick hug and kiss, I said bye to my mum's sister before stepping out into the blazing sun. As I skipped down the few steps from the veranda, I felt rather strange wearing socks and hiking boots in this weather.

"Take care, you hear."

She stood on the veranda watching me leave, and I replied by giving her a quick wave as I approached the mini-bus. It looked full up and I don't know why, but I was surprised by how many white people were on board.

As he saw me approach, the driver got out and walked around to meet me, and he could only be described as a man mountain. He looked like no man I had ever seen before and though I could feel myself staring at him, I couldn't look away. The men I had met back at home always tended to be too weedy or laden with a beer belly. But this guy could only be described as a tall, dark, broad vision of loveliness.

What would have been a baggy T-shirt on an average man was straining against his broad chest, distorting the word 'Canada' which was printed across the front in bold black lettering, contrasting with the white background. I couldn't help but marvel at his biceps, the circumference of which could easily match that of my thigh, which wasn't exactly skinny.

"G'mornin', miss."

"Good morning." I smiled back, noticing his perfect, straight white teeth.

"Yuh gwine sit up front wid me."

I clambered up into the passenger seat after he opened the door for me and exchanged greetings with the other holiday-makers before leaving them to chat amongst themselves. I just managed to turn in time to see my aunt nod curtly in reply to his cheery "G'mornin', Miss Yvonne."

"Yuh aunt ain't easy, you know," he said as he eased his bulk behind the steering wheel.

"I know," I chuckled guiltily. "But she means well, she's quite nice really."

"I'll take yuh word for it."

As he started the ignition, I took the opportunity to consider him further. His short, thick dreads stuck out all over his head, giving him a dishevelled look, but his face, complimented by a Roman nose, blemish-free smooth brown skin and full lips, was very handsome. He'd look much better without the stubble, though.

Now I've been known to fantasise about being with particular men, but that was usually after I'd been out on a few dates with them already and sex was in the cards. I found myself feeling quite self-conscious as I sat next to this man whom I was already imagining having sex with. It was unbelievable. Besides the fact he was probably quite capable of crushing me, I didn't even know him. Yet I could practically feel his strong hands caressing my body, manipulating me into the position he wanted in order to consider every inch of my skin.

I wondered whether he would be tender or quite rough but—as it was my fantasy—decided that he would be a bit of both, starting off gently before gaining pace and fucking me hard. I bet, like many black men, he liked a good-sized bottom, and I pictured myself on all fours in front of him, my cheeks in the air, my thighs parted, ready and waiting. He might even be a bit of a tease, holding himself back until I was begging for him to enter me. But even though he was rock-hard, he would summon some willpower from somewhere and merely rub his glans over my clit, feeling that I was dripping wet. I'd push my hips back eagerly and he'd finally grip my waist as he slowly guided his cock inside me, sighing loudly. The delicious feeling of his girth parting my lips would make me moan and throw my head back, causing him to slide his hands up my back before running his fingers through my hair, holding onto it as he slowly withdrew his cock until only the tip was inside me. He would make me wait, he would remain in that position for several long seconds before suddenly plunging his cock deep inside me, making me cry out as I felt his balls smack my pussy lips.

As he continued to hold my head back, he would lean over me and I would crane my neck to kiss him hungrily, eager to feel his lips on mine, to taste his mouth, to suck his tongue. I would be completely under his spell and he would be the first to pull away, leaving me hanging, not wanting the kiss to end. But he wouldn't give me a chance to protest before resuming fucking me, his long, slow strokes quickly turning into hard thrusts. He'd lean forward to rub my clit as he pounded harder and faster, his grunts drowned out by my increasingly loud moans...

"Yuh happy wearin' shorts?"

Before speaking, he had already turned the mini-bus around in the small area at the top of Hungry Hill in order to go back down the narrow gap, but stopped to comment on my attire.

"Yes, why?" I replied quickly, feeling rather embarrassed, as if he could somehow read my thoughts and could tell that there was a distinct dampness developing between my thighs.

"Dem mosquito an' beasts gwine eat yuh alive," he informed me, fixing me with his soulful, nearly black eyes.

"But you're wearing shorts too," I retorted, looking down at his own khaki cut-off combats. Despite the length of them, they had managed to ride up when he got behind the wheel and I got a glimpse of the firm thigh beneath. I instantly — and very vividly — imagined my fingers running along his smooth skin on my way to discovering how big he was. I could quite happily picture myself massaging my hands up from his bulging calf all the way to his thighs. I'd switch to using my tongue as soon as I got high enough.

"Yeah, but mi skin t'ick like elephant own and dey like new blood…sweet like nectar."

"I'll be all right."

"Yuh sure? Dem bite gwine mark up yuh pretty skin."

Conscious of all the people in the back waiting to go on a hike in order to collect photos that wouldn't get looked at, I assured him that I'd be fine and felt relieved that I had put some insect repellent in my bag. I didn't know what to think about the fact that he was checking out my legs or that he said I had pretty skin.

Despite the bad condition of the roads and the many hairpin bends, he drove fast and the wind whipped through all the open windows, creating an atmosphere that wasn't as stifling as I would have expected. Between the wind and the old school reggae that he only turned down slightly, we had to speak loudly to maintain a conversation.

"Jeanette yuh name?"

When he hadn't said anything in a while I'd assumed he was concentrating on the road, so was glad when he spoke as everybody else on the trip seemed to be part of a couple. Despite knowing that I'd probably feel a bit self-conscious after that fantasy, I preferred not to spend the trip on my own and, anyway, logically, I knew he had no idea what I'd been thinking.

"That's right, what's your name?"

"Mi call Wileman."

"Wildman?"

I knew that everyone I ever came across in Grenada had a tag name, which usually had something to do with their personality or an event in their life, but this one was unusual. It served to cement the idea in my mind that he was obviously a wild man in bed. No doubt he had women all over the island clamouring after him to experience the immense amount of stamina he looked like he possessed.

"Yeah, cos mi like bein' out in da bush, bein' wid nature." He smiled, flashing those teeth again.

"Okay."

"Plus, yuh don' think mi look wile?"

He ran his fingers through his dreads, grinning mischievously as I smiled back at him.

"Wha' part a Englan' yuh come from?"

"London."

He nodded knowingly. "Mi only been to sout' London."

"Really? Which part?"

"Brixton."

"Oh, I live quite near there…in Wandsworth."

He just nodded again, lapsing into silence as he beeped for the umpteenth time before taking another bend.

"Jus' a holiday yuh come for?"

I turned to consider his face before replying as I was sure he already knew the answer. News tended to spread across the island like a fire in a paper factory. But he just looked ahead, his bulbous bottom lip protruding slightly as he waited for me to speak. I would have liked to have leaned across and kissed it before gently sucking it into my mouth.

"Yeah, I just thought I needed a break."

"Mmm hmm." He fell silent again, allowing the chatter from the back of the vehicle to drift to the front.

I sat wondering what he would normally be doing on one of these trips. Would he be chatting to everyone in the back? Would he be singing along to a reggae tune? Would he have some other lone woman sitting next to him thinking about him much like I was? Would he be making advances? Who knew?

It was a gorgeous day, the cloudless sky was an amazing azure blue and I was having a mini-adventure. I only hoped it wasn't going to be too strenuous. I knew my limitations.

* * * *

After another twenty minutes of driving and ten minutes of walking, I was quite pleased to find that I wasn't as useless as I thought. We travelled in convoy, me powering ahead and Wildman bringing up the rear. I was amazed that within the short time the group of twelve people had been travelling, a few people had already started moaning about the heat of the dense rainforest.

The wife of one of my fellow adventurers was the worst culprit. Apparently sick of listening to her, he soon joined me at the head of the group, speaking to me in his soft, southern drawl.

"Wow, you've got so much energy, are you a runner?"

With that slow, syrupy accent, I was expecting a big broad JR Ewing type. But what I got was a skinny, rather nerdy looking white man.

I laughed at the assertion. "No, I can barely run for a bus."

"Well you look really powerful."

Never having been told I looked powerful before, I was surprised but appreciative. I thanked him for the compliment before we exchanged pleasantries as we walked in the humid shade of the tall trees.

I didn't get the chance to discover much about the genial American before Wildman's deep voice interrupted our conversation.

"Ai yo!"

The sticky heat had become too much for some of our number—lightweights—and a rest was required to enable them to recover. Those who were the most overcome sat under a tree, resting their backs against the thick trunk as they guzzled down water before resuming their complaints about the heat. Others milled around, looking up into trees to try to spot the birds that were producing the continuous song that seemed to follow us wherever we went.

I stood alone, having been abandoned by my new friend for the sake of checking on the condition of his wife, and wiped some sweat from my face with a flannel before taking a swig of water from the bottle I took from my bag.

"Yuh don' wan' sit down and res'?"

I nearly dropped the bottle and succeeded in dribbling some water down my chin and almost choking.

"Sorry." He smiled as he lightly patted my back, obviously amused by my coughing fit. "Mi nah mean fe scare yuh."

"It's all right," I replied when finally able to speak, wiping my mouth and wondering how many more times I was going to embarrass myself in front of this man. I wondered what we would be doing at that moment if we had been alone. I'm not sure I would have been able to resist him even if he wasn't interested. It wasn't standard behaviour for me to make a pass at a man when I had no idea whether he liked me or not, but I would make an exception for him. I would unashamedly fling myself at him and press against his chest until his arms folded around me.

Towering over me, he silently stood for a moment, smiling broadly.

"Yuh enjoyin' it so far?"

"Yes, thanks."

"Yuh nah 'fraid?"

"What should I be afraid of?"

"Sometime woman does be 'fraid a snakes an' lickle creatures dere about. But yuh real brave."

In order to look like the brave woman he thought I was, I smiled modestly and scanned the leaf-covered ground for any movement the instant he walked away.

Chapter Two

Though I was on the alert for the rest of the day, I didn't see any snakes. There were birds, lizards, monkeys, all sorts of creatures...but no snakes. Thankfully.

There were many more rest stops, some of which I was grateful for because after only about thirty minutes I started to flag. Wildman didn't seem to tire, he was clearly as strong as he looked. The defined muscles of his calves and arms rippling with every movement, he even carried the bag of some lazy tourist when the man began complaining that he was unable to go on. I now had no doubt about the power behind that body. He would keep me up all night and still be able to leave me begging for mercy.

In all it was a pretty good day, and I was glad I hadn't chickened out as I'd thought about doing several times. As we made our way back to the mini-bus I was tired, hot and sweaty, but satisfied that I hadn't made a complete fool of myself and didn't feel as if I needed an oxygen tank. That would be embarrassing at the best of times, but I definitely didn't want Wildman to see me struggling. He probably already thought I was a pathetic City girl who couldn't take the pace. It was inexplicable that I was seemingly incapable of thinking of anything else but him. Maybe it was the heat.

"Yuh enjoy yourself?"

"Yes, thanks, it was really interesting. Nice to see a part of the island that I haven't been to before." I happily took credit for Aunt Yvonne's idea rather than give a lame response.

"Good."

"What about you?" I asked after a brief pause. "Oh, but I suppose you must see it all the time."

"Yeah, but mi nah tired of it."

Eager to get back to the mini-bus, everyone else in the group had gone ahead of us once they knew where they were going. Wildman and I followed behind, him towering over me as we walked side by side. I kept attempting to take surreptitious glances at him to see the sweat glistening on his bicep, but he was so close to me it proved difficult. Just him being so close to me was enough to make my heart pound against my ribcage.

"Yuh in a rush fe get home?" he asked as the big white vehicle came into view.

I wondered why he was asking and briefly considered saying something cheeky like, 'Are you going to make me an offer I can't refuse?', but I decided against it on the basis that it was just too corny. "Um, no, not really."

"Okay, I gwine pass by da hotel firs'."

The journey to the hotel was much like the one to the mountain. Wildman was rather taciturn and I didn't want to seem presumptuous so only spoke when I was spoken to. It gave me an opportunity to get lost in my thoughts again, making my vulva contract by imagining him stroking it as we kissed.

As he pulled up outside the massive building, he assured me that he wouldn't be long. He got out of the mini-bus to help the other passengers disembark, many of them shaking his hand before trudging wearily into the comfort of the plush decadence that awaited them. With my head out of the window, I bid my fellow day-trippers a warm farewell while I watched our host out of the corner of my eye. He patiently stood talking to one of the tourists who wanted to chat, listening to the inane nonsense with good grace and responding when needed. Finally, the man ran out of words and followed the others inside, waved off by Wildman.

"Yuh ready?" He smiled, getting back into the vehicle.

He was still so cheerful. If I'd had to deal with a load of loquacious, complaining tourists all day, I'd be ready to kill somebody by the end of it. But to him it seemed like water off a duck's back.

"Yep."

Taking the tourists out of the equation served to loosen his tongue, and he was more talkative on the way back to Birch Grove. I felt more comfortable to ask him questions when he asked them of me. I discovered that, apart from running excursions for the hotel, he also did odd jobs for people, had travelled to most of the islands in the West Indies, lived quite close to my aunt and had a desire to visit Brazil.

My first thought was that the desire probably had something to do with the Brazilian ladies and their round posteriors, but thought he had that in Grenada already.

"Brazil? What appeals to you about Brazil?"

"Da wile life an' rain forest an' t'ing."

"Oh, okay." I had to stop being so cynical.

"So Fontaine is yuh family people?"

"Yep, that's me, Jeanette Fontaine."

"Mmm hmm."

"What about you? I don't even know your real name."

I clearly detected a mischievous twinkle in his eye when he turned to me and smiled. "I prefer Wileman."

The attempt at mystery just made me even more curious, but I didn't need to push him because I would only go home and ask my aunt. She knew everyone's business. She would know his real name and would be quite happy to tell me. It would be her cue for a good gossip, I would probably find out a lot more about him besides.

"Yuh seem like yuh like to explore."

"Do I?"

"Yuh was de only one nah complainin' 'bout da heat, and yuh seem fit, walking fast, ahead of everybody."

Fit? I knew he meant fit as in healthy rather than good looking, but I still felt as if the temperature had suddenly shot up.

"Well it was obvious it would be hot, so I can't complain. Anyway, I want to create some nice memories for when I'm back in the cold, sitting in the office all day."

"Yuh tryin' new t'ings."

"Exactly."

We sat in comfortable silence for a while, listening to the reggae tunes flowing from the speakers, occasionally punctuated by the voices of people on the street drifting through the open windows as we passed by.

"Yuh ever been fishin'?"

"Fishing? No, it sounds boring," I blurted out without thinking, immediately wishing I could take it back.

Far from being offended, he chuckled at my opinion. "I gwine make it interestin'. Yuh wan' come fishin' wid me tomorrow?"

After a few minutes of unnecessary persuasion, I agreed. His deep, rich voice was as delectable as a piece of good quality chocolate. If he would have asked me to rob a bank with him I probably would have said yes. Apparently, there was a river not far from where I was staying and, as I had no plans, we organised a fishing trip for the next day.

The brave man even agreed to pick me up at my aunt's, despite it being likely that she'd be home. Impressive.

Hungry Hill was at the top of a narrow road. In fact, it was narrow to the point where it was quite a hazard for vehicles to travel up and down it as they were always in danger of straying into the ditch at either side. To this end, I told him I'd be happy to walk the short distance up the hill if he dropped me off at the foot of it. But Wildman didn't even give my suggestion any consideration. He skilfully guided the wide vehicle up the narrow opening to drop me right in front of my aunt's house.

"Thank you very much. For the day and the lift home." I turned to him to smile warmly. I'm nothing if not polite and wanted him to know how much I appreciated everything he had done, the fact that he had looked after me and shown me a good time.

"Dat's a'right Miss Jeanette. I gwine check yuh tomorrow."

"Okay, I'll look forward to it," I confirmed, before attempting to get out in a ladylike manner.

I stood and watched him leave, feeling a strange mixture of sorrow and apprehension, sad that the trip was over and I wouldn't be seeing him again until tomorrow, but concerned that it would be a whole new opportunity for me to look like the prissy City dweller that many Grenadians imagine Londoners to be.

I envisaged him turning up with his dreads stuffed into a weird little hat, swinging a stinking tackle box with a fishing rod balancing on his shoulder. Sitting in front of a river for hours waiting for fish to bite wasn't my idea of fun, but he was good company so it might be all right. With any luck, he might get his shirt off and I'd get to see whether his chest was as sculpted as his arms.

"Y'ave a good time?"

"Yes thanks, it was really good." I joined my aunt on the sofa where she was watching an American soap opera, one of her favourite pastimes.

"Good…good."

She was engrossed, so I sat silently for a few minutes before getting up to go and take a shower. My movement triggered more questions as it took her attention away from her beloved soap.

"Dat big hardback somet'ing look after you?"

"Wildman? Yeah," I replied, carrying on to the bedroom. "He's taking me fishing tomorrow."

"Wha'? Wha' he takin' you fishin' for?"

It was difficult to tell whether the question was rhetorical or not, but I hoped it was. So I pretended not to hear. If she really wanted to miss her soap to discuss my plans she would ask again, but I preferred that she didn't. At twenty-nine, I was way past explaining my choices or asking permission to go out.

After quickly undressing, I made it to the shower without attracting any more queries and, thankfully, didn't hear anything more about it for the rest of the evening.

I spent a long time in the shower, imagining my hands were his as they wandered over my skin, causing a tingling sensation to shoot through my body when they lingered at my nipples, caressing and pinching them as I thought about how he would do it. My imagination was so vivid that it only took a few minutes of stroking my clit to make myself come, one hand braced against the tiles as I slid my finger deep into my warm cleft, trying to remain as quiet as possible as the water cascaded over my body.

I knew that asking my aunt his real name would result in another barrage of questions and I was just too tired, so I went to bed knowing nothing more about him. But I was well aware that my aunt was one of the most tenacious women ever created. I was sure she would continue her line of questioning in the morning and I'd get the opportunity to pick her brain then.

* * * *

As usual, Aunt Yvonne was already up when I woke, standing in front of the hob stirring a pan of bush tea.

"Morning."

"Mornin', Jeanette, you all right?"

"Yeah, I'm fine."

"I makin' your breakfas'. You need to fill you belly before you go out..."

Wait for it.

"...where you goin' again?"

Ta da!

"It's some river, not far from here, I think its Balthazar."

"Jus' you an' dat big hefty man goin'?"

I couldn't help but let out a chuckle. "Yes, just me and the big hefty man. Don't you like him?"

"I don' trus' him."

"Why not?"

"I jus' don't," she replied decisively, managing to be as cryptic as she was adamant.

It was pointless to try to pin her down to a reason, she probably didn't want to admit that she had formed an opinion of him on the back of a rumour, which was usually the case.

"Do you know his real name?"

"Hmm, Jackson...Jonathon, something so. 'E nah tell you?"

"He says he prefers Wildman."

"Well call 'im dat. 'E mus' wan' keep it secret so none of 'is women come after 'im."

This comment caused another laugh from me. She was probably picturing me going off fishing and being ravished by the big hefty Wildman. It made me determined to bring home some fish so as not to make her suspicious, and I knew that nothing would happen anyway. He was just doing his friend at the hotel a favour, making sure I had a good holiday. He had no idea what kind of debauched thoughts I was having.

Despite her mistrust, she didn't try to persuade me not to go or tell me I couldn't go, but I caught her looking at me strangely a few times, then denying all knowledge when I asked her what was wrong. Made uncomfortable by the attention and disappointed that she was unsure of his name, I left her to it as soon as I finished breakfast, retreating to the bedroom.

Though he said he would pick me up in the morning, I was well aware that time didn't mean much on this island and, for all I knew, he could turn up at four o'clock. With that in mind, I threw on a vest top and a pair of little shorts, tied my relaxed hair back in a loose bun, grabbed a book and sat out on the veranda.

I'm not entirely sure why everyone seems obsessed with keeping me in the shade, maybe they think I'm so unused to the sun I might get heatstroke and faint away. But I like the sun, I miss the sun, it doesn't often visit me in London, so I was determined to catch as many rays as possible. I managed to read a few pages before the beautiful, warm sun began demanding my attention and I sat in the plastic chair, angling my face to the fireball's rays, hopeful of deepening the colour on my face as well as the rest of my body.

I have no idea how long I was sitting there, but it seemed like only a few minutes before his deep voice called out my name.

"Miss Jeanette."

My eyes instantly opened, but I still had to blink a few times before I could focus enough to see Wildman standing at the bottom of the veranda steps, his red string vest making him look even broader than he did yesterday and enabling me to catch a glimpse of his developed torso.

"Oh, hello."

I jumped up, wondering how long he had been standing there and why he was empty handed. Where were his rod and his bait? His approach had been so quiet, I wasn't sure why I'd expected him to turn up in the mini-bus. I knew the river wasn't far.

"G'mornin'."

"I'll just go and put some clothes on," I said, apologetically.

"Yuh a'right as yuh are."

"Huh?"

"Only by da river we goin'. Da fashion show is nex' week."

Even though he was taking the piss out of me, I laughed. I couldn't help it, it was funny and he just came out with it as if it was the most natural thing to say. With a little wry smile on his face, he studied me with his deeply dark eyes until my laughter subsided.

"Okay." Though, in reality, I wasn't entirely happy about walking around with my thighs on show. "I'll go and get my bag."

"Wha' yuh need a bag for?"

I actually had to think about it. What did I need my bag for? I think I carried one around out of habit.

"Nothing," I shrugged, forced to admit the truth when confronted with the question.

"Mi 'ave everything yuh gwine need. Yuh aunt home?"

"Yeah...Aunt Yvonne," I called out from the doorway. "I'm going now."

She could have acknowledged me from where she was, but instead she left the kitchen in order to watch us leave.

"G'mornin' Miss Yvonne," he said politely, as soon as she came out onto the veranda.

"Mornin', Wildman."

"I gwine bring yuh niece back in one piece."

She smiled — unbelievable! "Mek sure you do!"

"See you later."

"Bye, take care."

I was very conscious of the fact he was watching me as I walked down the stairs to join him on the hot concrete path before we made our way down the gap. I didn't need to look back to know that she was standing there watching us until we disappeared from view.

Chapter Three

Initially, I felt quite uncomfortable, as if I was on show, not that I had that much to show. My breasts could be described as only a bit more than a handful, but the vest was still quite low cut, showing my cleavage, and the shorts were...well...short. After we passed and greeted several women dressed very much like me, I worried about it less.

Much like when he took me home yesterday, Wildman was a quality conversationalist—not too nosy, equally happy to tell me about himself as he was to discover things about me.

Though I had no idea where we were going, I felt quite safe with him, despite having only met him yesterday. Maybe it was because my aunt knew him, maybe because he was so big and could clearly protect me. Whatever.

"So yuh like to eat fish?" he asked, placing his hand on my back to guide me as we veered off the road.

The touch to my skin was electric and I actually had to think hard about how to respond to the simple question. Though his hand wasn't on my skin for long, I felt it long after he moved it away. "Yes."

"So 'ow come yuh never go fishin' to catch dem?"

Looking at him, I returned the mischievous smile that he directed at me as I thought about how to answer.

"Because I live in London, which isn't known for its fishing…and it's the land of the supermarket."

At this, he threw his head back and laughed, making his dreads shake about and catch the sun, which made them look brown as the rays shone through them.

"Well, I gwine teach yuh to fish in case yuh ever lost by a river an' yuh need to eat."

"Okay." I chuckled as we veered off the road and he led me down a gentle slope.

We walked deep into the bush, weaving our way through densely packed trees, and though I still couldn't see the river, I could already hear it.

"Right, yuh ready to prepare?"

"Prepare?"

"Yep, we need bait to catch de fish."

I didn't know how I was supposed to respond or what he expected me to say, so I just looked at him blankly. His eyes twinkled as if they had never known sadness. I was actually rather envious of his smooth skin, which looked like melted chocolate.

"Yuh mus' dig up some worms."

"Me?"

"Yep." He flashed me a wicked smile, pleased by my surprise, before looking around and locating a thick branch on the ground. "Here."

I don't know why I accepted the proffered branch, I had no idea what to do with it. I took it anyway and looked to him for guidance, waiting for him to explain my next course of action.

Seemingly relenting, he took it back and began digging in the heavy earth. "Okay, if I dig dem up, yuh mus' thread dem on de hook."

The thought of even touching a worm made me wrinkle my nose in disgust, causing Wildman to laugh at me. His gorgeous laugh made me smile and I could have listened to it all day.

In less than a minute, he was directing my attention to the earth he had turned over to show me the long, thin, grey worms that were to be our bait, wriggling about without a care in the world.

He handed me a small plastic bag that he produced from one of the pockets of his combat trousers. "Collec' some worms, nah."

I made an effort—I really did. I crouched down and looked at the disgusting little things but was loathe to touch them. Amused by my hesitation and, apparently, the look on my face, he told me that it was okay if I didn't want to collect them, I could bait the hook instead.

With thumb and forefinger—and great trepidation—I picked up worms until he was satisfied we had enough.

The way he narrated as I watched him make a rod, I wondered whether he thought I was actually ever going to make one myself. I paid attention in any case as it was fascinating and his voice was as gorgeous as ever. I watched the tiny lines around his eyes deepen as he concentrated on the task, squinting as he made sure the hook and line were securely tied.

Finally it was ready and we walked down to the river's edge where he directed me to sit on a big rock before he made me watch him thread the worm onto the hook.

"See, nothin' to be afraid of. Easy."

"Yeah, I'm still not doing it."

He laughed as he closed his hand around mine in order to lead me into the fast flowing water. His warm hand was so big that mine practically disappeared. I could feel a patch of calloused skin on his palm pressed against my skin.

"Where are we going?" I asked, incredulous, my buttocks remaining firmly on the rock.

"Da crayfish under dem rocks, dey nah comin' to us, we mus' go to dem."

I looked into his eyes as he spoke. I knew he was trustworthy and I didn't want to portray myself as a wimp — not any more than I had done already. Keeping a tight hold of his hand, I followed him into the river, the water reaching just above my knees, and could immediately feel the rocks on the river bed through my rubber flip flops, some sharp, some loose.

He was holding my hand throughout, but after the third time of nearly losing my footing, I was too scared and tried to loosen his grip so I could turn back.

"Wha's wrong?"

"I can't do it. I'm going to fall over."

Firmly gripping my upper arm, he pulled me to him and turned his back to me as he rested my arm on his shoulder.

"Get on."

I hesitated for a second before climbing onto his back, putting my arms around his neck and allowing him to give me a piggyback to the middle of the river.

The man was solid muscle.

His broad back could easily accommodate me, I probably barely registered as extra weight as he effortlessly waded through the water, one of his smooth thick forearms hooked under one of my legs wrapped around his waist. From my vantage point, I watched a bead of sweat form at his hairline before trickling down his temple and had to fight the urge to wipe it away. I couldn't believe I was on his back, very few layers standing between being skin to skin with him. He remained silent as he carried me to our destination, and I wondered how he would react if I kissed his neck at that moment. Maybe he'd be less outraged if I gave his biceps a squeeze, I figured I could probably get away with it. After all, I already had my arms around his neck, my breasts pressed against his back.

"A'right, here is a good spot," he confirmed, bending down to let me off, which I did reluctantly, standing on a smooth rock in shallow water.

"I gwine show yuh firs', then yuh gwine do it."

I nodded slightly, now actually quite eager to see what he would do in order to demonstrate what a good and willing student I was, wanting to improve the impression I was making on him.

With the rod in one hand, he used the other to move one of the smaller rocks we were standing by as he explained that the crayfish liked to hide in crevices. Satisfied with the small movement, he held the end of the rod and allowed the hook and worm to sink into the clear water amongst the cluster of rocks.

"Watch dis end."

I resolutely stared at the end of the rod, with no idea what I was supposed to be looking for, but I did it anyway. After a few minutes of nothing happening, I was about to ask him whether he was sure this would work, when the end of the rod was suddenly tugged.

Like an idiot, I gasped with surprise.

"When I pull it up, yuh mus' catch it, yuh nah."

"How?"

"Cup yuh two han'. As dey come out de water, dey drop de worm, so yuh haffi be quick."

"Okay," I replied to the earnest instruction as I saw the line get tugged again.

Slowly and smoothly, he pulled it out of the water to reveal a crayfish on the hook. I quickly shoved my cupped hands between the creature and the water, desperate not to disappoint my companion by losing the first catch of the day. Just as he said, it immediately dropped into my hands, which I triumphantly held out to him.

"Well done," he grinned, as he rifled through his pockets to find a clear plastic bag.

With my fingers curled around the crayfish, I watched him scoop up some water into the bag to put it into and, obviously not happy about being taken from its home and then ignored, the damn thing pinched me. I was so surprised that I started and nearly dropped it, but Wildman grabbed it in time and put it in the bag before he tended to me.

"Lemme see." He gently took my hand and considered the slightly injured finger. "Yuh gwine be fine," he confirmed before kissing it.

He kissed my finger! I couldn't believe it. His lips were much softer than I'd expected. I was sure there was a stupid grin on my face, but I tried to shake it off because he carried on as if nothing had happened, insisting that it was my turn. If the smallest kiss was capable of making me feel like that, who knew what else he could do? I wanted to kiss him back, though not on his finger. I wanted to wrap my arms around his neck and kiss his lips as gently as he'd kissed my finger. I wanted to kiss my way down his neck all the way to his hard chest.

We spent several enjoyable hours at the river and caught lots of fat crayfish. I even got the chance to tease him when one pinched him and he dropped it back into the river. When the bag was full up, he decided we should go and, on his back, he took me across to the riverbank. Much like the day before, I found myself quite disappointed that the fishing trip was ending and that I would soon be leaving his company.

"Now yuh know how to fish." He smiled as we made our way back to the road.

"Yeah." I giggled, looking at the bag of crayfish I was holding. "I'll have to find a river in London where I can use my new talent."

He smiled broadly before stopping dead in his tracks in the shade of the trees, the thick foliage serving to slightly reduce the temperature and humidity.

"What's wrong?"

"We haffi wait a while, rain fallin'."

Confused, I looked up at the sky through the sparse gaps between the trees and peered in the direction of the main road. The sun was shining.

"It's not raining."

"Is comin'…mi can hear it."

He leaned against a tree, smiling at the sceptical look on my face.

"Yuh nah believe me?"

I wanted to say 'no, you can't hear rain coming', but I had a feeling that if I did, I would end up looking stupid. I just shrugged and joined him next to the tree, waiting to see if he would be proved right. As we stood there, he gave me some ideas about meals that could be prepared with the catch and I teased him some more about the one that got away. Though I'd only just met him, I didn't feel any of the awkwardness I normally felt around strangers. There was no place in the world I would rather have been than standing there chatting and laughing with Wildman. Though he was easy to talk to, my thoughts left me feeling slightly on edge as if the longer I stood there the easier it would be for him to detect that I was lusting after him.

Within about five minutes of his prediction, there was a whooshing sound that gradually increased in volume until it turned into the steady, persistent patter of raindrops falling onto the leaves above our heads.

It was actually raining.

I stared at him open-mouthed as he grinned gleefully. "Yuh see?"

"Okay, I'll trust your word next time."

Still smiling, he nodded before we both fell silent, listening to the beat created by the raindrops.

It was as if the insects were trying to find some shelter from the rain, and finding my legs was a bonus, so I started to stamp my feet to try to get rid of all the sand flies and mosquitoes that were attempting to feast on my blood.

"Dem beas' bitin' yuh?"

Before I could reply, he had crouched on the ground and I didn't get a chance to ask what he was doing before he started touching me, gently running his big, calloused hands up and down my calves and ankles to dislodge any insects trying to take up temporary residence.

I stood stock still, thinking that maybe the right thing to do was to tell him to stop—after all, I barely knew him—but I didn't want to. His touch was electrifying and was causing reactions in parts of my body he was nowhere near. I actually found myself wondering whether he would move his hands up to my thighs and then wished hard that he would.

Someone must have been listening, because the next moment he was slowly standing up and running his hand up my thighs as he did so, brushing his fingers between my legs. That was all it took. A shockwave shot through my body that instantly caused moistness to develop between my legs.

He met my gaze as he slowly straightened. My mouth fell open, craving for him to kiss me. As if reading my mind, he grasped my neck, forced me back against the tree and crushed his lips against mine, snaking his tongue into my mouth in search of mine as I ran my fingers through his soft locks, holding onto him, wanting the kiss to be even deeper than it was.

I gasped into his mouth as he suddenly, grabbing my bum, picked me up and pressed my back against the tree as he leaned against me, enabling me to wrap my legs around him and feel his hard cock eagerly prodding my pussy through our clothes.

Tightly gripping his broad shoulders, I submitted to the pleasure of the deep, passionate kiss as I tightened the grip of my legs around his waist, grinding against the twitching cock that I so desperately wanted to fill me.

We were both breathing so hard that we were drowning out the sound of the rainfall, and as I began to rub my covered pussy against him, he began to moan into my mouth. Even as I was kissing him, I couldn't believe it was happening. The thought of me being able to get this big, powerful man so excited was so deliciously thrilling that I could take it no longer and dragged my mouth away from his to hoarsely whisper in his ear.

"Please...fuck me."

Breathing hard, he looked into my eyes as he quickly pressed his lips against mine before releasing his tight grip of my behind, lowering me to my feet and hurriedly undoing his trousers. Following his example, I quickly undid my cut-off denim shorts, but, distracted by the release of his twitching member, stopped before I had the zip all the way down. I was actually scared. Not only was his cock long, but it was the thickest I had ever seen and I was seriously afraid it would hurt me.

He kissed me as he slid his hand into my open shorts, pushing aside my cotton thong and quickly finding my throbbing clitoris to rub it with small, circular strokes, making me even more wet than I was. I reciprocated by gripping the beast that he kept between his legs, sliding my hand up and down his shaft. As he skilfully stimulated my clit, he used his free hand to push down my shorts and thong in one go. He only needed to move them a short way before they fell to my feet of their own accord, as if they knew how much I wanted him and were keen to get out of the way, knowing they were merely a hindrance.

His touch was so good that I was barely concentrating, but he seemed to enjoy it. He made a growling noise from deep in his throat as he pulled away from the kiss, running the tip of his tongue over my swollen lips before straightening up and looking at me through hooded eyes, watching my reaction as he plunged his finger deep inside my wet cleft. I moaned as my body jolted, causing my back and shoulders to scrape against the rough tree bark as he pushed my legs further apart with his foot.

Bending his knees until we were nearly face to face, he must have seen the slight panic in my eyes and kissed my lips.

"Don' worry."

Looking into each other's eyes, I gripped his shoulders as he guided his substantial member into my eager, wet pussy. For a moment, I couldn't breathe. A moan caught in my throat as the anticipation of feeling him inside me was finally being satisfied. Tightly clasping my bum, he lifted me with ease, held me against the tree and, breathing hard, slowly slid his cock out of my hungry pussy before plunging it deep inside me.

"Oh…Lord….yeah."

I dug my nails into his shoulders and wrapped my legs tightly around him as he slid deeper inside me, then pulled back slightly. I know he was watching me, but with my head back and eyes closed, I was lost in the pleasurable haze that resulted from being filled so deeply, disbelieving that I took the full length of him.

Before long, his solid chest pressed against my breasts and I screamed as he rammed the remaining length of his cock inside me. I had never felt anybody so deep. I was panting hard as my heart pounded against my rib cage and, as if trying to pull him closer to me, I slid my arms over his shoulders and dug my nails into his back.

I had never felt so much ecstasy so quickly. If there were awards for sexual prowess, Wildman would easily take first prize. His face was buried against my neck as he began slowly working his hips, gently gliding in and out of the slippery crevice that opened up to accommodate him.

I was gone. Lust and sensual pleasure took over and I had no idea how long he was smoothly sating my desire. I was brought back to my senses as he began grinding his hips faster, making his balls swing against me. He began to grunt as he pumped harder, increasing his speed, and kissed my neck as he detected I was coming to orgasm.

I could barely breathe, my throat was so dry, but all I could think was that I didn't want him to stop, I felt as if a dam was about to burst and engulf us both. His breathing quickened, he dug his fingers into my butt cheeks, I couldn't believe he was moving so fast, fucking me so hard, his balls slapping against me, the volume of his grunts increasing.

The gradual waves that I normally experienced didn't make an appearance. The orgasm hit suddenly, making me wrap my arms tightly around his neck as I screamed and my body trembled. Still hard, he reduced the speed at which he was thrusting into my contracting pussy and, after a few minutes, pulled back to look at me. He kissed my lips before slowly withdrawing his cock until just the tip was inside me, and continued to gaze into my eyes as he stabbed the full length of his shaft as deep as he could, making me cry out while I felt his flesh undulating as he pumped his hot cum into my crevice.

We remained there in a tight, sweaty embrace for a few long moments, both exhausted and enjoying the heat of the other's body.

Eventually, too tired to hold them up, I unwrapped my legs from around him and he gently set me down on my feet.

"Yuh a'right?"

"Oh…yeah," I breathed, a stupid grin on my face, leaning back against the tree.

We silently looked at each other for a while, both considering what had just happened.

"We bes' go back down to da river…I don' wan' yuh goin' home smellin' like sex."

Nodding in agreement, I took his proffered hand and followed him back the way we had come, only then noticing that it had stopped raining and wondering when that had happened.

Only after we had washed and were on our way back to the main road did another realisation hit me.

"Do you think anybody saw us?"

"Nah, nobody 'round 'ere."

He sounded confident so I just hoped he was right and tried to put it out of my mind.

We didn't say much to each other as he walked me home, we didn't need to. I did have the urge to run my fingers along his glistening bicep, run my tongue along his strong neck, slip my hand down the front of his trousers, kiss him passionately, just touch him, but I didn't act them out. If someone saw me, my aunt would know before she even saw me.

Thankfully, she wasn't on the veranda when we got back. I'm not sure my conscience could have stood up under her scrutiny.

"Well, Miss Jeanette, yuh real brighten my day."

I could only giggle like a teenager.

Taking hold of my hand, he took a quick look around before kissing it and then my cheek.

"I gwine see yuh soon."

"Okay."

That was it, the full extent of our conversation before he turned to walk back down the gap. Only as I stepped up on the veranda did I realise that I had all the crayfish and had assumed that he would be taking some for himself. I turned, intending to call out to him, but found myself just watching his impressive frame as he strode away. Before disappearing from view, he turned and looked in my direction, flashed me a smile and then he was gone.

As I turned to go into the house, I prayed that my aunt wouldn't notice anything strange about me and acted as casually as possible when I found her in the kitchen.

"Hi, I'm back. Look." I immediately held up the bag.

"Hello...whoy! You get nuff a dem. I gwine make soup wid dem."

I breathed a sigh of relief as I left the kitchen, happy that she was occupied with the crustaceans, and hurried to take a shower.

Every time I thought about him, about how he was so deep inside me, it made me smile. By nightfall, my pussy was gently pulsating, giving clear instructions on what it wanted.

Although the warm tingle felt good, it also worried me because I had no idea when, or if, I would see him again. I didn't know his real name, where he lived, his telephone number, nothing.

I went to bed wishing I'd told him that I would only be on the island for another five days. The sex was amazing and I didn't like the idea of going home without seeing him again.

Chapter Four

Two days had passed and I was starting to get worried. I was yearning for a man I barely knew and didn't know how to contact. Just in case he passed by, I only took a quick trip to Grenville because I couldn't think of an excuse when my aunt asked if I wanted to go with her, and I stayed home all the next day.

I knew I could ask her, or any of her neighbours, where he lived — everybody knew each other — but if I suddenly started asking questions, people would get suspicious and might work out something had happened between us.

Evening fell on another day and, with Aunt Yvonne at bingo, I was alone, sitting on the veranda where I had stayed for most of the day, trying to decide what to do and hopeful of seeing him walk up the gap.

Each time someone passed by, I greeted them warmly even though I was becoming increasingly despondent. I gave up my vigil with the arrival of the car that dropped my aunt home.

"Hello, did you have a good time?"

"Yeah, but mi nah win not'ing."

"Aww, next time," I consoled, even though I was actually feeling more sorry for myself.

"My frien' 'ave a good idea about de day before you leave, she t'ink we should 'ave a cook-up on de beach."

"Mmm, that sounds like a good idea," I replied absentmindedly.

"Okay, I gwine start organisin'."

After a last look at whether anyone was coming up the gap and seeing no one, I followed her inside feeling more wretched than I had felt in a long time.

* * * *

Frustrated, I roughly pulled on my bikini bottoms after having already put on the top, glanced at myself in the mirror, then slipped on a t-shirt and shorts. It was just my luck to find a man who had given me the best sex I'd ever had, and then not gotten an opportunity to see him again. Bloody typical!

I was leaving tomorrow afternoon and would be at the beach all day today, so I resigned myself to the fact that it wasn't going to happen. I wondered whether he'd had his fill and was finished with me. I was so disappointed that I would have liked to stay at home and sulk, but my aunt had invited many people and the cook-up was, effectively, in my honour, so I tried to ignore my feelings and enjoy the day.

It *was* a beautiful day, there would be lots of food and drink, maybe that's how it was supposed to be—go home with memories of one great passionate sexual encounter. It definitely wasn't something I'd be able to replicate when I got home—the environment or the man—so maybe I could just recall it the next time I found myself enduring sex with a guy who couldn't boast of the same talents as Wildman.

The veranda was packed with numerous pots, tubs, bags and containers waiting to be loaded onto the truck that would be coming to pick us up. As usual with these things, there was an open invitation so I expected to meet many people I'd never met before. It might be fun.

Only fifteen minutes after I got ready, the truck arrived, complete with blaring soca music. I avoided all the fuss of loading the beach related paraphernalia and went outside when it was done to find there were a few people sitting in the back.

I greeted the group as a whole and the replies merged into one, with the exception of a deep voice that stood out from the rest.

"G'mornin', Miss Jeanette."

In the corner by the cab sat Wildman, one sculpted arm stretched out along the side of the truck. I couldn't climb up quick enough.

Shyly, I smiled at him before sitting in the space in front of where his arm rested, disappointed that I wasn't in a position to shove my tongue in his mouth.

"Jeanette? You don' wan' sit in the cab?" my aunt asked after locking the front door and approaching the truck.

"No thanks, I'm all right here."

Nodding, she got into the front.

I was elated and did my best to keep a straight face when, at various times during the journey, his fingers outlined shapes on my back, teasing me with his light touch and sending a wondrous feeling shooting through my body, making my nipples tingle. I could feel them becoming erect and prayed they wouldn't show through my clothes. We barely spoke except to exchange the same pleasantries as the others on board, and still I felt as if everyone was watching us, that they all knew what we'd done. However, whenever I was brave enough to look around, all I saw was people taking part in their various conversations or watching the world go by, not paying us any particular attention at all.

I couldn't wait to get to the beach. I hadn't been to Bathway in so long, I couldn't remember whether it had any areas that were sufficiently secluded to enable us to get any privacy. I could only hope.

The long journey seemed to take no time at all and I found it easy to slip away with Wildman when the others were deciding where to set up the fire for the massive pot in which the food would be cooked.

Initially, so as not to arouse suspicion, we sat together in the sand a little way from the spot that was eventually chosen, where everyone could see us.

"Yuh did start worryin'?"

Thinking that saying 'yes, I desperately want you to fuck me before I leave' wasn't appropriate, I just smiled shyly and shrugged.

"I been real busy—nuff tourists just fly in, but mi wan' see yuh jus' before yuh leave, so yuh 'ave some nice memories to tek home." The man was a mind reader.

"Thank you, that's very considerate." I grinned before listening to his plan for the next day.

He wanted me to sneak out of the house, before dawn, and meet him so he could take me to his place. Just the idea of carrying out his plan was exhilarating and I was instantly turned on by thinking about what we could get up to. Not bothering to think about whether it would be possible or what my aunt would do if she caught me, I agreed. It had to be done. There was no way I was going to let this opportunity pass me by.

"Let's go in da water," he said, taking off his vest.

"Do we have to?" I was enjoying lying there in the sun, talking to him, daydreaming about the next day, wondering what would happen in the confines of his house, whether his stamina would be too much for me.

"Yuh at de beach, yuh mus' let da water touch yuh skin."

"I can't swim."

"I'll look after you," he said, helping me up before watching me, with a twinkle in his eye, as I undressed to my bikini.

"Mmm," he looked at me approvingly before we walked into the sea.

I waded up to my calves before he turned his back to me and firmly held my legs after I accepted the piggyback, taking me further into the water. I held him tight, relishing the feel of my skin against his and running my hands over his biceps before squeezing them as soon as the water provided sufficient cover. In response, he ran his hand back along my thigh and pulled aside the material covering my pussy and slid his finger inside me.

I tightened my grip on him as I sighed contentedly in his ear, desperately wanting to kiss his neck but scared someone would see me. Instead, I rubbed the heel of my foot against his growing erection, longing to feel it inside me.

"Is there anywhere we can go?"

"Nah, too many people around, yuh cyan't wait 'til tomorrow?"

"I don't want to," I whined.

He chuckled before squeezing my buttock and grabbing my arm to pull me around to face him. Quite fearful of the depth of the water, I kept a tight hold of his shoulders and looked into his eyes as he slipped his hand back into my bikini bottoms, rubbing my clit as he squeezed my bum with the other hand. Despite my fear, I felt compelled to touch him and wrapped one arm around his neck, my face close to his. I slid my hand into the elasticised waistband of his long shorts, smiling as I wrapped my fingers around the stiff cock that had made me so euphoric.

I wanted to kiss him and glanced up at the shore, noting that we were quite far out, but still not prepared to risk it. Instead, I firmly glided my hand up and down his shaft, gradually increasing in speed as his finger pumped harder into my pussy, his thumb massaging my clit.

I moaned with the pleasure he was making me feel and I watched as he soon closed his eyes, grunting as I continued to work on his cock. Within a few minutes, he leaned his head back and groaned as he climaxed, his body shuddering. He looked so good. I cupped his balls in my hand and gently squeezed them as his ecstasy subsided and he pumped his finger faster, determined to bring me to orgasm. He didn't have to work hard.

"Oh…oh." Conscious of where I was, I had to restrain myself for fear of being too loud, but the intense feeling didn't change. My nipples tingled as my pussy muscles tightened around his finger.

When I opened my eyes, he was looking into them, smiling.

"Yuh too bad, yuh nah!"

I laughed as he grabbed my waist and pushed me past him to get on his back, which I duly did, holding tight as he returned me to the shore.

The rest of the day was brilliant. I had a lot of fantastic food, had a few drinks and had a few laughs with a lot of nice people. I had a really good time. I couldn't be sure that I would have had such a good time if Wildman hadn't been there, but that wasn't something I had to worry about because he was there. There were times throughout the day when we would catch each other's eye and exchange small smiles, leaving me wondering whether he was as excited about our imminent encounter as I was. It was impossible to tell, but I figured that it was his idea so he must be keen. Unable to help myself, I continually took sly glances at him whenever I could. His body was a work of art…I couldn't wait to get on it.

* * * *

Although I knew I should have done, I didn't go to sleep. I probably wouldn't have been able to if I tried. I had told him I would meet him at the bottom of the gap at three a.m., and the anticipation was enough to keep tiredness at bay.

As soon as the time came, I successfully crept out of the house without alerting my aunt and quickly trotted down to find him standing exactly where he said he'd be.

With nothing resembling streetlights, I couldn't see a thing and he held my hand in the darkness while I wondered how he managed to see where he was going. We didn't say a word to each other during the short journey, a situation that I was quite pleased by—we knew what was going to happen and were comfortable enough to walk silently, each of us contemplating what was to take place in the rest of the morning.

It didn't take long to get back to his small, wood built house.

Inside his bedroom, he put on a lamp and I stood looking up at him in the soft light, waiting for him to make a move.

"I bin lookin' forward to dis."

He tenderly removed my clothes before laying me on the bed, considering my naked body as he undressed, not revealing any embarrassment at the fact that I was watching him closely, my heart pounding harder with every item of clothing he discarded.

His body was magnificent and I turned on my side as he joined me on the bed. He mirrored my posture and pressed his lips against mine as he pinched my nipple before running his hand along the contours of my body, squeezing my bum when he reached it.

When he had taken off his trousers and revealed his hard cock, I had already started to get wet, but just the touch of his hand on my skin and I was drenched. Maybe it was because he had gone from standing up in front of me to lying down next to me. He was within my reach and I couldn't wait, I didn't want to wait so, gently pushing his shoulder while I continued to hold his gaze, I straddled him as soon as he was on his back.

As I pressed my pussy lips against his twitching cock, his hands flew up to my breasts, squeezing them before pinching the hard bud at the tip. Raising myself, I took hold of his cock and guided it inside my wet pussy, slowly swallowing it as I softly moaned, gazing at him. He completely filled me. Grinding against him, he was deeper than he had been the first time, the feeling was incredible.

As I began rhythmically rocking my hips, he sat up and wrapped his arms around me, holding me tight as he sucked my nipples.

It was as if we were in perfect harmony, each body knowing what the other wanted, helping each other experience wave after wave of pleasure. Despite the hour, it was still hot and we were both sweaty, but it wasn't enough for us to pull away from each other. Over the next few hours he made me come countless times.

The man had a phenomenal amount of stamina and just as I thought I couldn't take any more, he would manoeuvre me into another position and start all over again until we were both exhausted, our lust temporarily quenched.

It was a struggle to leave when the sun began to rise, not only because I didn't want the experience to end but because I was so swollen — my lips, my nipples, my breasts, my pussy — but I still felt good. It was all worth it.

Watching him walk away after he dropped me home, I just felt strange. It was a mixture of sadness, introspection, gratitude and fulfilment, but I was certainly happy that I had been able to see him again.

I just managed to make it back into the house before Aunt Yvonne started to stir. I could have gotten a couple of hours of sleep, but I didn't. I finished packing as I pictured the last few hours with Wildman. It was like I could still feel his hands on me, still taste him, still feel him filling me. I was quite sure I would never feel muscles like that again, never have sex like that again, never meet another man like him.

After finishing the task, I pulled off the jeans I was wearing as I tried to decide on my outfit for the flight home, and sent something skidding across the floor and under the bed. Puzzled, I got down on my stomach to retrieve it and found it to be a small piece of dark wood carved into the shape of a fish, with the words 'gone fishing' carved into one side. Chuckling to myself, I turned over the smooth trinket to find the initials 'JF' on the other side.

It was so sweet and thoughtful. I don't know when he must have slipped it into my pocket, and now I couldn't even thank him. I quickly stashed it in an inner compartment of my flight bag, not wanting to lose it.

* * * *

Having thought I saw Wildman amongst the crowd at the airport, I spent so long telling myself that I had just imagined it that my musings made the eight-hour flight seem much shorter. I was soon sitting on my sofa, continuously turning the wooden fish over in one hand while I held the phone in the other, trying to calculate what the time was in Grenada.

Wildman had made a point of taking my telephone number before I left his house, but now that I was home, back to my real life, I convinced myself that it was just for show, so that I wouldn't think he had used me. He didn't even have a telephone line connected at his house. Why would he bother calling?

Eventually, I estimated it to be about four p.m. and figured it was safe to make the promised phone call to Aunt Yvonne to confirm that I got home okay.

"…and you did 'ave a good time?"

"I had a fantastic time." I smiled.

"I'm glad, you gwine 'ave to come down more often."

"I definitely will."

"Good. Oh yeah, I fin' out da hefty man name…it's Johnson Franks."

"Johnson Franks," I repeated, tracing my finger over the letters etched into the wood.

"Yeah, I fin' Wileman suit him better."

"Yeah…Wildman. Wildman *is* good."

I smiled to myself, wondering why he hadn't mentioned we had exactly the same initials, I thought it was an uncanny coincidence. It was only then that I knew for sure that I wouldn't again leave a gap of several years before I went back to Grenada. Just the thought of the wondrous Wildman was enough to make me want to immediately book the next trip out there.

"I hear he travelling next mont'," she said earnestly, as if imparting actual knowledge rather than gossip.

"Really? Where?" I asked quickly, not bothering to do the sensible thing and ask how she had found out.

"England, I t'ink…"

I didn't hear anything else she said as I traced my thumb over the initials carved into the side of the little wooden fish.

I was useless for the rest of the day. All I could think of was seeing him again. I was elated at the thought that he would rather see me than go to Brazil and could practically feel his hands, and the anticipation of feeling the real thing instantly made me wet.

MISERY LOVES COMPANY

Ellen Ashe

Dedication

To those I have lost yet still watch from beyond the veil.

Chapter One

"How long you reckon to stay, honey?"

Lola smiled politely. "I paid for the cabin for two weeks." Despite the forced etiquette of her smile, her tone hinted no such decorum. The man's marauding stare raking up and down her body made her skin crawl. It was likely unwise to antagonise him, especially seeing they were in the middle of nowhere and if he actually tried something on her no one would hear the scream. Still, Lola wasn't about to back down even though the caretaker's sneer turned into a snide chuckle. "So two weeks it is," she added stiffly.

"Yeah, okay," he said, as though he held more than the key to the cabin. He leaned against his rusty half ton and stuck a hand-rolled cigarette between his knife thin lips, cupping the match so that the stiff wind off the water wouldn't kill the flame. He sucked the cigarette hard, blowing smoke out his nose like an infuriated dragon. It evaporated within seconds. The smile, such as it was, suddenly dropped off his face. "But I highly fucking doubt it."

He stood there, staring at her with black, sunken in eyes. Obviously he wanted her to squirm. It worked. Her skin crawled. She was very anxious for him to give her the key and leave.

"Why would you say that, Mr. Darci?"

Those beady eyes shifted sideways to the cabin. Then back. His mouth pinched a grin. He thrust his hand in his jean's pocket and passed over a key. When she reached out to take, it he took hold of her wrist. He squeezed.

She stiffened, fearing the worse.

No one will hear me scream.

His breath stunk of nicotine. Intermingled with it was a whiff of whisky. "Don't touch the typewriter," he growled, barely moving his lips. He hadn't blinked. "Its former owner wouldn't like it."

"Why?" The question fell out, not because she wanted this conversation to linger but because she was frightened while trying hard not to show it.

He leaned forward, his mouth against her ear. "Don't say you ain't been warned, Honey."

He let go of her wrist, wrenched open the door to his truck, and hopped behind the wheel. The window was down. He shifted the gears. The truck slowly rolled backwards. "Bottle of Jack in the fridge," he said, the cigarette hanging out one side of his mouth. His voice cracked with sinister laughter. "You'll need it."

As defiant as she'd tried to be, a deep foreboding, like a fever, flushed her flesh. Was it the old man's sadistic mannerism? He was playing some pathetic head game on her, perhaps? Why? She was a recovering alcoholic, but he had no way of knowing that. He was a complete stranger.

Strangers. Strangers had been known to force themselves on other strangers. Sometimes they even killed other strangers just for the thrill of it. The old man was getting a sadistic pleasure out of scaring her. She knew his name—the property's owner had told her the caretaker would meet her with the key—and they were both strangers. Lola sighed. Even those we think we know, those we even profess to love, can turn out to be complete strangers.

A long shadow over the freshly mowed lawn coaxed her to hurry inside the cabin. She took her suitcase from the backseat of her compact, leaving the sketchbooks and pencils until last.

The step leading up to the veranda squeaked beneath her foot. A mouse scurried under the pile of wood within reach of the front door. The screen bumped slightly in the growing breeze. And just as she pushed the key into the lock and heavy sigh drifted over the back of her neck.

Mournful. Desolate. Isolated.

She froze for the moment, letting a wash of misery pass through her and sink from her heart to her stomach, weighing her down like a heavy black stone. And then she softened. The melancholy flowed through her, taking nothing of her soul with it as it passed, which gave her the distinct sensation this sadness was not her own.

She was, however, being watched.

She turned.

Nothing. Nothing except the stabbing thrill of the unknown in her gut.

She'd expected the sensation to be excitement—at forty-something, she had few passions left, except maybe her drawings—nothing she saw or thought or felt or did seemed new or exhilarating. Addiction had a profound way of killing enthusiasm for life. But that was behind her now. This was new. This being alone in a cottage on a lake beneath the mountains for two weeks of delicious isolation, rejuvenation, and creation—this was new.

Life was slowly beginning again.

Her decision to be here was unprecedented in its spontaneity. Being organised and methodical in making plans, she could never remember acting wildly on a sober impulse. Never. So she'd had expected the freedom of the wilderness to touch her in some mysterious and exhilarating way. But what she sensed had nothing to do with any of these expectations. This was far more profound, almost sexually passionate because…the unexpected resided here.

And still, someone was watching her.

She *felt* eyes on her. She scanned the winding lane that led to the main road. Might the caretaker have parked his truck just out of view and snuck back, to wallow in success of seeing her paranoia flare up because of what he'd said to her? Yellow and orange leaves fluttered in the gusty wind, an orchestra of blended noise. A few zigzagged to the earth. Nothing else stirred.

"Mr. Darci?" she called out. She was both fearful and disappointed when he didn't answer. If he wasn't there then who was? Or, the other explanation might simply be that neurosis had flared up, miscuing her senses. Perhaps the months of psychological counselling had achieved nothing and her fears were what she was.

Stupid bitch. Lola lowered her eyes. Married for how long and that was the last thing he'd said before leaving. The memory cut into her heart almost as severely as when it had actually occurred. A disastrous spiral of anxiety, years of medication, alcohol, more depression had all taken their toll. She'd lost her life for something she just couldn't control, for something no one seemed to understand.

"I can pick myself up," she whispered. "I am not stupid. I am not a bitch. My therapist said I have the strength and I have the strength." Saying it aloud was supposed to help build her self esteem.

It didn't. A solitary tear trickled down her cheek. Her demons had followed her here. And they were watching her.

"Go to hell," she cried out. "I'm not afraid any more!" More defiance. She jabbed the key into the lock. Another passionate sigh exploded in her ear. With it she was certain there was a soft touch, lips on her cheek. She should have been startled. Instead she was aroused. Deeply.

Her senses tingled. My god, this was new! And exhilarating!

She left the key protruding in the lock, like lovers, frozen in the moment of intense intimacy.

Lovers. She turned, taking steps in slow motion towards the narrow wharf that jutted out into the lake. Water lapped against the wooden posts. She stopped at the very edge, kneeling on the ragged wood and breathing deeply the sweet autumn air. The sun was setting over the ridge of ancient mountains. The water shifted, a lulling sound. Tranquillity. This was a world far greater than herself and despite her inadequacies she was welcomed here. Inadequacies meant nothing here because being alone meant she wouldn't have to be judged. She allowed herself a few moments of composure, to become one with what was surrounding her, to allow a deep blinding desire to assert itself. Meditation. A desire for wholeness. If she couldn't find peace here she wouldn't find it anywhere.

She would not judge herself. Not anymore.

"I will survive," she whispered with a contented smile.

As she spoke a swirl of wind picked up water, the twisting funnel dancing over the surface. It lasted for mere seconds before dissipating as mysteriously as it had formed.

Wonders beyond her existence.

Birth of renewal.

Lola rose, concentrating on getting settled into the cottage.

* * * *

The interior was stark. One room. A worn couch, table, two chairs, a bureau, and a dusty rug covering the centre of the bare board floor. A single bed was next to the wood stove against the far wall. It squeaked menacingly when she sat on it, testing the mattress. The quilt that draped the bed was handmade, its colours as muted as the shades of brown that made up the room. Above the bed hung wind chimes. She reached up, smiled when they tinkled. She wondered why they were inside and not hanging in the breeze on the porch.

There was no breeze inside. "You're in the wrong place," she whispered. These words seemed to express her general attitude towards life. Loneliness crept through her, so sudden and so stark she wavered, thinking perhaps she should turn and run.

But she paused, and as she did, comfort came to her in the form of an embrace. Arms, thick and strong circled around her torso from behind and as the dream wrapped her in safe warmth she tipped her head back. Breath moistened her ear, full lips pursed against her skin, hair fluttered against her cheek. She touched the hand that had begun to explore her breast. Her eyes drifted longingly across the bed.

"Yes," the voice in her ear seemed to moan, as though echoing her sudden desire for intimacy. And as she turned to kiss her new lover, to embrace him fully, she staggered to nothing but cold air.

Her suitcase, perched by the door where she had dragged it, fell over with a thump.

For several moments she simply stood. She neither rationalised nor fantasised. One step at a time. And the next step would be making the room comfortable.

She lit a fire in the stove, the warmth mixed with the scent of burning wood. An oil lamp on the table would be her only other source of light. This was from choice. There was a lamp run by generated power, but since she was going to enjoy the full sensation of living the rustic life she made a conscious decision not to cheat by flicking a switch. Everything she sensed would eventually seep through into her drawings. Every sense added to the passion of what would become artistic creation.

Passion. She caught herself stopping, waiting for the ghostly kiss against her ear, the hand on her body, yet all had gone silent. Ghosts. The word made her smile. She was left to explore, alone. That was the reality of it despite her imagination.

There was no typewriter.

Unless it had been stored in the back pantry. She pulled aside the curtain. Shelves were well-stocked with non-perishable goods, but no typewriter. A worn paperback caught her eye — The Edge of Sanity by Jamie Hill. She smirked, considering the irony. The cover depicted a woman who had her back to what appeared to be a haunted house.

"You look good for being on the edge," Lola snuffed. Normally she didn't read romances. But where she was, what she was doing, that wasn't normal either. This she might read. For company, if nothing else.

She put the book back on the shelf, returning to put more wood into the stove, and light the lamp.

The room seemed to take on a glow. Heat and light transformed the starkness into—dare she use the term—cosiness? Warmth. Delight. It was time to replace the darkness of depression with light and warmth. It was time to walk away from any edge.

She placed her suitcase on the floor beside the bed. Then she went back outside to collect her art supplies. The haunting cry of a loon echoed over the lake. The wind had died. The surface of the lake was a mirror. The leaves were no longer dancing.

If not for the chill in the air, she might have opened her sketchpad and started drawing there and then. Quickly sketching the scene for posterity. If not for the chill, she might have luxuriated, at the very least, in the soft bewitching of this motionless silence. Perhaps it was the profound stillness that caused her gaze to suddenly shift towards movement—what seemed an anomaly in serenity—a shadow, at the very most, indistinguishable except for its human form. Movement was swift, away from her, under a tree, around the side on the cottage.

One leaf had started vibrating. One single leaf on one single tree in the yard, shaking all alone on its dried up stalk. Rattling almost. Like a macabre wind chime. The significance of what might be the supernatural escaped her for the moment. It was far too eerie to sink into conscious reasoning.

"Hey!" she demanded. It was a flash of bravery between surprise and anger—the place that cushions each side of fear. She ran to the edge of the building, not slowing to consider this could be a foolish act. If the intruder turned on her no one would hear her scream.

Yet there was nothing.

Her heart pounded in her ears.

Nothing. Even the leaf had fallen still. Abruptly.

She backed away, quickly gathered what was left of her belongings from the car, and once inside the cabin, she bolted the dead lock.

She sat, wearily, on the edge of the bed. Surprise and anger had drained away, leaving the sharp sting of alarm. What had just happened? She cocked her head, listening for any indication the intruder might still be outside, stalking around the cottage, waiting for the chance to defile her.

Her imagination spun wildly. Always she assumed the worst. And even though her inner voice tried to sooth away her paranoia, anxiety had lifted its ugly head. The flame had grown and there was virtually no way she could stop her thoughts. Unless she took the medication. Unless she passed out from alcohol.

"Why do you do this to yourself, Lola? Why?"

She bowed her head to sob. An honest outlet of emotion. She'd come here to escape anxiety, to rest, to create and it was ruined. Ruined! It just wasn't fair. Nothing was fair.

Long after the tears had stopped she sat, a prisoner to a parade of memories. "Think of the good things," she said aloud to herself. "Think of the happy times."

And there were many to think about—mother teaching her to bake, to sew, to knit, to read; father teaching her how to gut a fish, how to pitch a tent, how to cook a meal outside over an open fire. She thought of family vacations, celebrations, laughter, reunions. The voices and the laughter were both gone. Lola had to concentrate to remember the voices and sometimes she couldn't remember. And although these memories were supposed to comfort her during episodes of darkness, they didn't. She grieved for what was lost. "How can remembering something that was so wonderful make me feel so miserable?"

She wanted simple answers. She never got simple answers. The depth of emotions was a swirl of complication. All on it beyond her control.

"All I want is to be in control, and the harder I try, the worse I get," she'd confessed.

"It's not easy," her therapist said. "But we'll get through this."

Maybe, Lola had sulked to herself. *If I wasn't such a stupid bitch.*

The fire had all but burned out. She got up, stiffly, opened the windowed door to put on more fuel and watched as the flames flared to the dry kindling. She briefly debated heating some water to make a cup of tea.

"Bottle of Jack in the fridge." The caretaker's voice resonated through her mind. She had been sober for over a year. Alcohol was a road she could never allow herself to travel again.

Unless she wanted to die. Slowly.

"Don't touch the typewriter."

Her eyes lifted. There in the corner of the ceiling was a hatch. Beneath it the floor was bare. There must have been a loft, accessible by ladder perhaps. Not that she was curious or energetic enough to find out tonight. In daylight she'd explore.

She finally dismissed the day's events, including the old caretaker, the wind funnel on the lake, the mournful sigh in her ear, the shadow, the cup of tea. She stretched out on the bed, folded the musty quilt over her shoulders and slept.

* * * *

She woke cold. Through her restless tossing and turning, the quilt had fallen to the floor. It seemed that all night, numbed with fatigue and unable to fully wake, her dreams had tormented her with an incessant clicking of a typewriter. She'd heard the frantic ticking, would turn to shake herself awake in order to fully grasp what the sound could be but was unable to do more than to sink back into the dream where the shadow slouched over the typewriter, its arms shaking to the rise and fall of fingertips on the keyboard. Her dreams kept logic thrown asunder. Maybe her dreams worked as a filter, discarding the uncertainties of the preceding days.

Now she was awake. And cold.

Rubbing her fingers together, she stepped outside to get firewood. Heavy white frost blanketed the lawn. The lake was still. The air was fresh. This was paradise. A new day.

She smiled. "Release the pain," she chanted several times. "Release the pain and begin again." She gathered a few sticks of wood and went back inside.

Lola stoked the fire. She poured bottled water into an oversized tin cup and dropped in a teabag. It would brew while the surface of the stove heated. The memory of her father drifted through her mind—how he'd smiled over to her as she'd sat beside him on a log and he'd taught her how to make tea, to cook on an open fire—and for one precious second she remembered the sound of his voice. There was no grief. Only warmth. Perhaps she was healing. Her time, alone, in the wilderness, might turn out to be the best therapy of all.

She went through the small pantry and out the back door. An outhouse. Not her favourite part of the rustic experience, but there had to be some disadvantages to pioneer living.

"Take the good with the bad."

On the way back to the cottage, however, her blood ran cold.

Crack.

She froze where she stood, a tide of anxiety washing over her. Someone was here, around the corner of the cottage.

Crack.

"Who's there?" she called out, but her mouth was dry and her words had virtually no strength. One foot in front of the other she slowly inched across the white frosted grass.

Crack.

Not a shadow this time. A man. His back was to her. Thick black curls hung over his wide shoulders. He was wearing only a pair of jeans and work boots. The tanned skin on his back was moist despite the early morning's cool air. The axe rose over his right shoulder and every muscle in that shoulder flexed as the axe blade smashed into the wood. He straightened, wiped his brow, or so she assumed from where she stood, and then he positioned another log for cutting.

She had never seen a body as perfect as this except in a magazine. The flow of muscle, the narrowing torso, thick thighs and the firmly curved ass that filled the tattered jeans and as her eyes lifted he ran his fingers, front to back, through his hair.

Her reaction was instant. An unexpected stranger had caused alarm but now her thrashing heart had nothing to do with fear. Raw hunger. A surge of heat rushed through her pelvis. A teasing contraction. She was engrossed in a raging battle between mind and body. Her body wanted this man deep inside, writhing over her, a hard penetration. As her eyes raked over him again her mind concurred. But what if he was a depraved villain, what if he knew she was here alone and meant to defile her with violent acts? What if he thrust his hand over her mouth so that no one would hear her scream? The thought of danger only fuelled the sexual fire. Her groin flexed. She was wet.

His breath billowed like steam — heat on cold.

Lola was speechless. Despite her burning desires she needed answers. A small voice whelmed up that an unexplained danger was too serious to neglect. Had the cabin been double booked by mistake? Had someone asked this man to check on the place? Make sure she had enough supplies to be comfortable and safe?

He didn't take another crack at the wood. Instead he straightened, dropping the axe. It hit the earth with a thud. She expected he'd sensed her presence and would turn to see her standing there. But he didn't. He seemed thoroughly intrigued by an unidentified object out in the water. She squinted, wondering what it was that had captured such profound concentration. Or, he was waiting for her to speak.

"Hello?"

He had to have heard her. Her voice was strong now. Yet, except for his shoulders' rise and fall to heavy breath, the steam of it billowing into the cold air, he stood unmoving.

She inched closer. Hardly a dozen paces separated them when again she was violently assaulted with a rush of fanatical desires. Madness — she could do anything, would do anything, for him, with him. It was as though she approached a figure in a dream, a man who could push her into an abyss of passion, into a place where only heightened sensations produced by such a dream could prevail. With each step her arousal grew. She, too, was a disconnected figure in the same dream.

Her senses turned inwards. Love, empathy, pity. Awakening. Pleasure.

He lifted his arms slightly, tilted his chin towards his shoulder. Not to meet her anxious gaze but to listen. He was listening to her pounding heartbeat. His nostrils flared. Lips parted. His eyes closed. Suddenly he moaned. Pain or ecstasy, she couldn't discern.

Still, she moved closer. Her hand extended. She was shaking with exhilaration. She had to touch him.

"Yes," he sighed, knowing.

Her fingers made contact, a feathered touch on his waist. A ripple shuddered through his torso. Energy tingled up her arm. She lifted both hands, clasping his solid waist, drawing her body closer, pressing her cheek between his shoulder blades.

His skin was soft, moist, warm. She kissed the small spot next to her mouth — the taste sweeter than wine. He reached around and hugged her into his back. His head tilted, hair cascaded over her face. He smelled as delicious as the fading autumn leaves beneath the sun's dying warmth.

She was beyond herself. Spiralling rapidly away from all inhibition.

She had to feel him, truly *feel* him. A wash of sensuality pooled in her groin. Responding to its feral appeal she moved her hands across his chest, tweaked a hard nipple on a solid mound of muscle, and she smiled as he flexed beneath her caress.

"More," he said, his arms strengthening, luring her into the promise of extreme pleasures.

She lowered her hands over the silky hairs on his stomach, stopping where flesh met denim, tugging playfully at the edge. He swayed, parting his legs. Then he took hold of her wrist.

"Touch me," he pleaded, while thrusting her palm firmly over the stiff bulge. As though fearful she might deny him his plea he kept his hand over hers, pushing so that she could not refuse this invited exploration. He gyrated to the pleasure it gave him.

"Touch me, harder." The plea changed to demand. He sounded like a man who gave orders naturally and had others follow those orders without hesitation. There was no escaping. She didn't want to escape. She liked being told. By him.

She had succumbed to temptation and the euphoria was taking control. She would do all he asked.

A stranger. She was dancing with a stranger who was dark and very possibly dangerous. No one would hear her scream. Even this thought added to the mystique, doubling her urges.

So she griped his groin through the denim. And bit into the flesh on his shoulder.

A whirlwind of motion, blocked sunlight—like a shadow falling over her eyes—and a forbidding rampart of muscle was suddenly thrust against her. When she stopped moving she was on her knees, submitting again to the persuasion of what was lurid, her lips parted to welcome the sticky sweet wine of lust. He had her hair firmly entwined in his fingers, and he directed her forward to his unyielding erection, perfectly aligned with her mouth.

Without hesitation she took him, obeying his command to be pleasured. His grunts of appreciation were short, sharp. His thrusts forward were similar. His palms heated her jaw, his touch gentle now because he knew she intended to do as he wanted, that she would not leave, that she would carry out her silent promises. She felt, too, his eyes on her, the same eerie sensation of eyes watching when she'd first arrived. There also was the heavy sigh that pursed into her mind, only this time she was fulfilling an act where this response was justified.

She clutched his hips, shuffled in, and took him deeper, twirling her tongue around the mighty girth, waiting anxiously for the tightening, the gasp, the short prelude to his release.

A stranger. No face. No name. No history. No past or future. Just then and now.

His thighs flinched. He sucked in a long hard breath of air. He clawed her scalp, death grip over her temples. He plunged himself into the back of her throat.

And screamed in agony.

He pulled away from her so abruptly she fell off balance. Before she had the inclination to lift her eyes, to question what had gone wrong, he turned away.

She swiped the back of her hand across her mouth, the taste of him lingering on her tongue. "Why?" she asked, her voice hoarse. "What's wrong?"

He wanted her pleasuring; she was willing, able. Yet he baulked?

His only reaction was to stride, rapidly, in a straight path across the lawn towards the short wharf.

"Hey—wait a minute," she yelled, rising in a panic and stumbling after him, unable to keep up with his frantic pace. He reached the wharf first, lifted his arms over his head, palms together while still in full stride and without any hesitation dove head first into the water.

She stifled a shriek with her hand and raced over to where her lover had jumped.

"Oh my God," she whimpered, a terror like none other, paralysing her mind with white searing heat, blinding her to rationale. There was no ripple in the water where he had jumped! There was no man swimming in the icy cold water. There was no sign that anyone, other than her, had walked across the lawn.

"Oh my God," she repeated, shivering uncontrollably. She turned, a full circle, but the man, who'd moments ago been her passion's desire, was nowhere to be seen.

Edge of sanity. Perhaps she had stumbled closer to it than she thought.

"Who are you?" she whispered.

The answer came in black emotion. Misery. It sloshed through her, twisting her heart in an agonising jolt. A sudden rush of bitter air, a sensation of total destitution, neither of which she could explain, enveloped her. And yet, she felt a warm glow of empathy. Affiliation. Kinship. And this alone pushed the terror away. The shivering ended abruptly.

She knelt, lowering her fingers to trail through the water, to create a ripple. The reflection of her own face shimmered, her features distorted. She couldn't see herself clearly. She never could. Beneath the reflection she was certain a dark face peered back up to her.

"Please," she said softly. "What are you afraid of?"

Her heart opened, like a vast ravine. Her fingers continued to trail the water's surface despite the burning cold.

"Don't be afraid of me. I want you. I want you to want me. Again."

The memory of him wrapped around her mind. The feel of his muscle beneath skin, the sweet scent of his flesh, the sound of his feral moans, and the taste- oh! She struck the tip of her tongue under her lip. The taste of a man. Of this she would drink freely. Forever.

"Are you lonely?" she asked. "Are you hurt?"

She couldn't be certain whether she spoke to him or her shifting reflection. She was certain, however, that the subsequent voice didn't come from inside her mind.

"Yes." Barely a whisper, wet against her ear, but she heard.

He's reaching out to me. Because no one else heard him scream.

Her mind didn't entertain the idea he wasn't real. He was real because she'd felt him. She'd tasted him. He was real because he'd turned his attention solely to her.

She had no idea what had brought him here, or when, or what had happened. All this was a mystery but she understood the dark cloak of depression and how it muddled all other sense. Including the instinct to survive.

She understood that here, in the quiet autumn morning, they shared a common bond.

"Let me help you," she said calmly, as though an old and treasured friend stood by her side. "I can comfort you if you give me another try." In the moment, she completely forgot her own self obsession, her own struggle from the depth of despair — it was a hopeless battle anyway. "I can comfort you," she said, her eyes darting up and down the shore, over the glassy surface of the water. And she marvelled at the growing strength of her newly formed conviction. "I need to help you because I can't seem to help myself."

Yet no answer was returned for this, her generous offer.

"It's okay. In your own time." She smiled as she turned to go back to the cottage. Somehow time no longer had any consequence.

Chapter Two

If she had been in a proper state of mind she would have packed her few belongings, gotten back in her car, and driven away. A normal, intellectually sound-thinking person would agree that such a logical conclusion was indeed apt. But by running she would rob herself of what might be one last chance to heal. Once inside the cottage she squared her shoulders, a physical manifestation of her determination to be strong.

The caretaker knew this cottage had been touched by an anomaly. He knew! That's why he doubted she could stay her for the full two weeks. Another reason not to doubt her sanity. Another reason to stay.

Her eyes drifted to the square door in the ceiling. A rope dangled from it. An invitation to discover him. He had heard her plea to help him because she was certain that rope hadn't hung there the night before. He wanted her to go and see what secrets rested above.

She tugged it. The door dropped. A steep set of steps lowered.

She gazed up into the dusty hue. There was some natural light—a window obviously—yet the unknown was still daunting. She remembered her restless dreams, those dreadful sensations of abject helplessness of being caught between sleep and wakefulness, and the distorted sounds that caused her heart to thrash with fear, her flesh to sweat. The typewriter. The keys had sounded all night long.

Evenly she took the steps, crawling, using her hands to hang onto the higher steps as though it was a ladder more so than a set of stairs. She pulled herself up through the opening and sat, peering into the muted corners of the loft.

There, beneath the solitary round window, was the typewriter. It was a testament to an era long gone. Large and cumbersome, its rounded black keys must have taken quite some effort to use. Especially if one was a dedicated author.

Lola inched towards it without getting up. Papers were strewn across the uneven floorboards. She picked one up. MISERY LOVES COMPANY. Typed over and over and over. Each page was the same. One piece of paper still in the typewriter had something more printed there. She turned the wheel, rolling the paper up.

MISERY LOVES COMPANY by Daniel Stone

"Daniel," she whispered. His name was Daniel.

She closed her eyes, remembering precisely the image of the man with the dark curly hair who was cutting wood, the one who had instantly become a lover, the one who possessed her so violently she was powerless without him. She remembered, too, the sense of loneliness that had emanated through her when she'd first arrived. The despair. Perhaps intermingled with the sorrow was his embarrassment that she knew he was in pain. Perhaps this is why he'd run from her, why he couldn't reveal his face.

Daniel. Knowing his name gave her the liberation of spiritual intimacy. Her heart seemed to soar.

Then briefly, suddenly, something touched her on the lips. A sweet strong fire flashed through her breast. Her heart skipped a beat and she heard her name being whispered as if by magic.

"Lolaaaa."

But when she opened her eyes reality swallowed the mystical encounter. She was alone in the loft with the typewriter. The fluttering kiss had fallen into the past with her growing collection of memories.

"I shall sketch you," she said. "I'll prove to you that what I saw was strong and handsome. Daniel? Would you like for me to do this?"

"Yes." So faint, yet a puff of breath was against her cheek.

"Oh," she sighed, in wonderment to the gentleness of it.

She slipped carefully down the narrow steps and took out her sketch book. She'd made a promise. She would keep it because she knew all too well the sting of a promise broken. She knew he'd felt that sting as well.

Her pencil, curiously, was merely a conduit, sweeping over the heavy paper, rapidly creating the figure that had been burned like a photograph within her mind's eye. Black hair curled over the shoulders, strength of muscle beneath the flow of brown skin. She drew him as she sat in the late morning light on the step, barely glancing at the page, instead watching the lake. Watching the lake as he'd done when she'd come up behind, when he was chopping firewood.

And when her pencil stopped moving, she studied what she'd created and was pleased. Except, a difference. In the picture, she'd drawn his face, shifted to the left, glancing back at her. There was a half smile on his mouth. His eyes were narrowed, as though, despite the smile, suspicion of her very sex was what haunted him most. Yet his fierce handsomeness was caught.

She was pleased with her work.

"Is this you, Daniel? Is this truly a reflection of you?"

She placed the sketch against a post. A mouse scratched under the woodpile. Leaves fluttered in a burst of warm wind. She lowered her head a moment, resting her cheek on her knees. He was a colourless image, black and white and shades in between. He wasn't real. He couldn't be real. And she hated herself for doubting.

"Lola."

Something brushed into her hair, a stray strand that had caught under her collar. She lifted her fingers to clear it away. A hand enclosed her wrist.

She couldn't speak.

He sat beside her, holding her wrist, his dark eyes staring at the scar slashed across the white skin. A vein under his eye twitched, voluptuous lips pinched together. He said nothing. His one quick nod denoted he understood. He brought her wrist to his lips, kissing the scar, pressing the newly made spot of wet skin into his cheek. The moment lingered. Her heart surged. He closed his eyes and drew an extended breath.

Then he pulled a clump of his hair to one side, exposing his thick neck, the skin permanently bruised, a narrow blackish blue laceration, under his chin and ear.

A shared cry for help.

Their affinity confirmed.

She didn't explain her scar. He didn't speak of his. There was no need.

They exchanged glances. His dark eyes shimmered as he peered to her. He kept holding her wrist in his cool hand. She felt his powerful masculine seductiveness. She felt his need and ached to verbalise her desire to fulfil it. Instead she leaned, slow motion, towards him. In response his lashes fluttered, his lips parted, and he accepted her gentle kiss.

It struck her with sheer bewilderment how profound and how primeval she felt. He was a stranger, a handsome unearthly man who'd cast a powerful spell over her sensibilities. Between them they shared a few dozen disjointed words. Yet the longing for physical warmth was mutual, the need to spiritually unite profound. It was both beautiful and terrifying.

"Cold, Lola," he whispered, his lips still on hers. "I am so cold. You are warm. You are the light through my darkness." His words were so soft they were barely distinguishable.

But she heard. The quiet scream. She heard and understood. "I'm here now."

"I did a terrible thing. I cannot be forgiven. The cold. It is my condemnation." He shivered. A tear streaked down the side of his nose, lingering on his lip. She brushed it away with her thumb. And she kissed the small spot where the tear had rested.

"Don't leave me," he said. "I can't be alone anymore." His shaking hands took hold of her. She trembled, too. She wouldn't leave. Deep in her soul she knew she couldn't leave.

From that moment on she couldn't exist without him. She wasn't strong enough to be alone. He was here for her. She had come to be saved. By him.

They were for each other.

She took a strand of his hair within her fingers, leaned, and coaxed his kiss to explore the curve of her throat. He reached for her, working his hand under her shirt, taking her breast fully in his huge palm. She inhaled sharply, pushing into his touch, floating to the prelude. His breath caught when she hummed a note of gratitude.

"That feels so nice, Daniel," she whispered into his ear. "You feel so nice."

His tongue trailed a thin ribbon of wet heat down her throat. She arched, giving him accessibility to suckle her. He tore her bra to one side with a vicious wrench and pulled her nipple into his pursed lips. He sucked fiercely, an unbreakable connection while his tongue lavished a flood of heat. She cradled his head, whispering words of praise into his hair, wincing to both the ecstasy and the pain of his persistent attention.

"Let's go inside," she invited. "Let's go inside and make love to each other."

A shriek. "Lola! No!"

The sky seemed to break, as thought silent lightning cracked reality.

She startled, lifting her forehead from her knees where she sat on the step. Her neck was strained and her back ached. Her head was muddled. She'd fallen asleep, but for how long, she couldn't be sure.

Beside her were the sketches. It was all she had of him. He wasn't real. Except, her breast was exposed. The skin was moist from where his mouth had been.

"Daniel? Don't leave me. Please, please don't go!"

The wind had risen, and clouds obscured the sun. She felt the cold, his cold. She was dejected, utterly alone. Miserable. She snatched up the sketches, cradled them to her breast and wept.

* * * *

The afternoon passed away. There was nothing she could do, and nothing she particularly wanted to do. Her mind and her body both were numb. She did, however, have strength enough to watch the shifting surface of the water and wait for Daniel's return. Occasionally, she whispered his name, her voice floating with the wind. Leaves fluttered. More fell to the ground. The air was sweet. So, too, was the tender memory of him. His voice. His kiss.

Yet, what if he was only an apparition, a figment of her broken imagination? She'd been with him twice, in waking dreams. A tauntingly delicious hallucination. A repercussion of a mind thwarted by chemicals. There could be no other explanation. She had to resolve herself to the fact that although she had come here to regain her sanity, this place was somehow dragging away what little she had left. Triggering illusions. Pushing her farther towards the edge.

He'd been here once. He'd rented the cottage, to get away from his past, to write in solace. This must have been true because he'd left his name in the typewriter, his mark within the world. Then he'd found no peace. He'd tried and failed. And then he'd disappeared.

"What happened, Daniel? Tell me your story."

Maybe time had twisted, showing her rare glimpses of what was. Or he was still here, but neither of them permanently shared the same space. Her mind spun with inconceivable possibilities, none of which made sense.

"Talk to me," she shouted. She felt free to do so because no one would hear her voice. Not even if she screamed. She opened her arms, moved in a slow circle. "Take me, Daniel." Her shrill voice crossed the lawn, the brunt of it directed towards the cottage. "Let us be together, two halves, made one." She cracked a laugh of nervous excitement.

She scarcely felt the ground beneath her feet as she made her way back to the cottage, so heavy-laden were her thoughts of him. She made a fire without feeling the warmth, ate without tasting, and found the bottle of Jack.

Clean and sober for over a year. She'd kept a job, an apartment, a quiet life. Temptation never left her side but for the sake of her job and what was the thin thread called reality, she'd stayed away from all the sinister pleasures that might lure her back into peril. It was different here. No one would know if she stole the touch of an old pleasure. Just one. Temptation was a sweet kiss.

"Nightcap," she said aloud, unscrewing the bottle cap. She filled two shot-glasses. "Join me, Daniel," she said lightly. "Let's make a toast to survival. Let's tempt one another." She downed the drink in one, throwing her head sharply backwards. It stung her throat. She put the glass down on the table.

The other was also empty.

"Lola."

She bit into her bottom lip, forcing a scream of frustration to remain lodged inside her throat. "Daniel." She spoke to the vacant chair. She spoke to what wasn't there except in pathetic dreams. She spoke to fantasy. She begged for hope. "I could love you if you let me."

A faint tinkle. The chimes over the bed danced. Her heart pulled.

He was listening.

"I was a coward. Only cowards try to..." Her voice trailed as she dropped her gaze to her wrists. "I guess we were both cowards. But we have each other now. We can comfort each other."

One more drink.

"I'll accept you for what you are if you accept me. I don't care what terrible thing you've done. It's gone, passed away. We deserve another chance. Don't we?"

The chimes over the bed fell silent. An elongated exhalation filled its place.

With that she could stand no more. She went to the bed and undressed, dropping her clothes in a heap on the floor. She crawled over the bed, resting on her side, arms lifted. She wrapped her fingers around the head post.

"Daniel?"

The chimes rotated in small circles, the music faint.

"I'm closing my eyes. I'm waiting for you."

The bed squeaked. A weight sat against her leg. She heard his breath, laboured, forced, uneven. Still she kept her eyes closed.

"I cannot be forgiven." His voice was throaty, as though a pressure restricted his larynx. "I could not find a light."

His palm rested on her upturned hip. The thumb stroked the fine hairs on her naked skin.

"I had no one to turn to," he rasped. "No one to help me. No one to hear me scream." The thumb flexed harder. "I was alone. I am alone. I will be alone."

"No more," she said.

"There is Hell, Lola. This is Hell."

"No, baby, not anymore."

The weight of an arm pushed against her turned hip, a hand strummed her throat. Hair passed over her cheek as moist lips lulled heavy sighs into her ear.

"I was betrayed. Anger stole my mind. I didn't stop being angry until my revenge was finished. I came here to hide and to write and to forget. I couldn't find solace. I can't forget. There is no peace here. Only regret. Only death. Hell."

Slowly she moved her arm, caressing his hair, coaxing his face to hers. In the dim light she saw his dark eyes shimmering.

"Daniel, I want to take away your hurt." She twisted fully into him, pulling his hair. "Make love to me."

A shudder of relief rippled through him.

His weight rammed against her. He was the source of an all encompassing river of passion flowing through her, and her only thought was to drown in him, to give her energy to him, then overcome him with her heat. He kissed her ear, her neck, her chin, her nose. He smothered her with delicious tenderness. She spoke his name, her tone filled with wonderment and love. And she wrapped her arms around his neck, keeping his naked body solidly within her grasp. She would not have him vanish again. She could not!

"I could love you so much."

"I could love you, too," he said softly.

He circled her wrist with his fingers. She strummed the line beneath his ear.

Her sigh was swallowed by his. He kissed her as none other, bathing her mouth with his tongue, forcing himself to squeeze tightly against her. She tugged his hair. He smelled of the warm autumn earth. His weight was upon her, all the while smothering her with the rapid wash of his mouth.

She made no effort to resist. His passion took away all thought. She was released from herself, free, uninhibited. She was only vaguely aware of how his hands worked over her body. Then with a feral growl he hoisted himself up between her sprawled legs. For an instant it seemed he had abandoned her but when she opened her eyes she saw he had crouched, kneeling, his gaze transfixed on her sex. He grabbed his cock, shuffled in closer, and patted the tip between her soaking lips. Suddenly his eyes lifted to hers.

They widened. With a mighty heave he lurched inside her body. She flinched to the intrusion, her internal muscle contracting around his mighty girth, a flush of fire exploding through her head, and he watched her face with searching eyes, as though feeding on her every reaction.

"Yessssssss," he hissed. He gyrated violently, an animal possessed, and she cried out from the shock of his force.

A smile crept over his mouth. "Beautiful," he whispered, his torso slowing. "So beautiful."

She circled her arms around his hard shoulders, coaxing him to lie over her. "Come here," she pleaded. He did as she asked. Locked together as lovers. He swayed over her, the flow of his spine like a rippling serpent. Euphoria. The dance consumed her because his body was comfortably inside hers. Fully. His lips on her mouth, a ceaseless stream of kisses. She inhaled his breath. And his moans.

"Don't leave me," he pleaded. "Please, please don't ever go."

Still their bodied flowed together. Her response was without thinking. "Never, my darling. Never. I promise."

The chimes above them vibrated.

If there could be some mystical way to crawl deeply into the heat of his chest she would have. She'd have lost herself inside his strength and become one with his enormous bulk. His fingers dug into her shoulders, his grip tight, severe. She sensed he was hanging on to her as fully as she was to him.

"I need you," he moaned. "I need you to find me in the darkness."

"Lover," she returned, her lips pushing into the damp skin on his throat.

His thighs constricted in developing urgency. The power of them reigned supreme over her. Deep in his throat she heard, no *felt*, a feverish, feral howl. It vibrated through her, heightening her arousal into sheer fire. He pummelled harder, lost inside his own need, oblivious to anything beyond satisfying his primal urge.

She bounced into him, crying out from the pleasure of his dominion. She pushed her palm on his hip, a request for him to dive deeper inside her body even though he was as buried as deeply as physically possible. His girth pressured the sides of her. His violent plunging was bearing the hysteria of desperation. Frenzied desperation. An insatiable hunger. Still, she had to have more. He was releasing her with his love making and oh! The freedom.

"So good," he puffed and then sucked a long breath of air, as though with difficulty.

She weakened abruptly. Rapid ecstasy stabbed and eddied through her.

His arms tightened suddenly, pushing her breasts up into his chest. His forehead fell to the pillow and he lurched. "Yes," he cried, a strangled weak voice. "I have found my salvation."

The chimes fell silent.

Her fingers trembled as she combed them through his silky hair. She thrust her face into the curve of his neck. His heart pulsed. He was so warm. She tasted salt. A lover's spice. Her fingertips ran down the smooth skin of his back. She cupped the flesh of his buttocks. Then she ran her nails up his backbone.

He shivered. She felt his curled lips against her skin and she smiled. It was a pleasure within pleasure to be this happy, to make him happy. To be this liberated. He moved his hips. He was still thick, hard. Wet.

"Lover," she said. "My lover. I found you."

He froze. A tremor rippled through him, as though he was stifling a cry of pain. He moaned a sad desperate sigh, an unfulfilled yearning, twitched as though he was no longer in control. A long breath exhaled. Seconds shifted but he didn't inhale. His whole body had gone...limp.

Stoic emotion swept over her, to protect, to cherish, to love unconditionally. She squeezed her arms with an all mighty strength, holding him tightly. She kissed him savagely, not knowing what else to do. Yet he was without breath, without pulse, without heat. And with revulsion she detected the sour scent of death.

"*Lola!*"

She bolted straight up, the sheets wet with sweat. The room was dark. A flash of lightning threw a quick eerie glow throughout the cottage.

"Daniel!" she screeched, but there was no answer.

No one heard her scream.

Her tongue was thick. The taste of whisky was on her lips. Her stomach wrenched. She staggered to the door, threw it open and fell, naked, into the rain. Crouched on all fours she gagged, her throat stinging with bile. Then she collapsed into the cold earth, wishing it would simply open up and swallow her whole. Thunder rolled above her.

She had finally fallen into her saviour's arms and he was Madness. Not Daniel. Not the strong, wanting lover she needed, but insanity. Nothing was real except this Hell she had allowed to possess her soul and destroy her spirit. There was no getting out. No recovery. No saviour. No light.

Without understanding how, she had twisted across the damp grass, clawing her way towards the wharf. Her muscles ached, her skin erupted in violent shivering. "I am half dead now," she screamed, hearing the water of the lake slosh against the wooden structure. She laughed, a type of hysteria setting in. "I might as well finish it off." Hot tears blinded her. Her hands were bleeding. "Do it right this time. Just do it."

Yet, folded half over the edge of the wharf, half over the edge of sanity, she studied the water in the dull light of the moon, hesitating. The storm had passed and the calm around her had slowed the storm inside.

She gazed down into the shifting surface of the dark gray water. She laughed when the ripples swayed aside to reveal a man's face, strands of black hair entwining with the waltzing reeds, squinting eyes peering back up at her, blackened lips moving to soundless pleas. She laughed because it wasn't there. It couldn't be there. And even if it had been there, a body submerged, and she was to scream in terror because of it, no one would know.

He opened his arms to welcome her.

She pushed air from her lungs with a mighty heave and rolled over the edge.

She didn't even scream.

But she never hit the water. Arms pulled at her, enclosed her into a warm pulsating chest, cradled her head against a strong shoulder. She was carried across the yard. She faintly heard the screen door bang. Then her head was lowered onto the pillow, the quilt draped over her body.

Then the familiar voice came. "You touched the typewriter, didn't you, honey?"

There was the stench of alcohol intermingled with a whiff of tobacco.

The edge of the quilt was tucked under her chin. A finger glided over the curve of her jaw. She was far too fatigued to respond. Or care.

"All right, honey," the voice soothed. A hand stroked her hair. "The rules have changed, though. There's no running away. He won't like that. His type expects promises to be honoured. Loyalty. Family motto." Laughter. "You be a good girl now, y'hear? Make sure your new man is well satisfied."

She didn't understand. She didn't try.

The wave of blackness took her into oblivion.

Chapter Three

Her first memory was that the typewriter never stopped clicking all night. The second was that she had dreamt of father, smiling at her as they cooked a meal over an open fire. He'd patted her hair and told her to be a good girl.

She rubbed her forehead. It ached. Her palms were cut. Dirt, grass, dried blood. Her body was filthy. Her mouth dry. "What did I do?"

She shivered, getting up awkwardly to dress, and to make a fire. The bottle on the table was empty. Another full one sat beside it. Did she drink all that then retrieve another? No wonder she hurt, her recollections foggy.

Except for him. Daniel. She stopped and turned around to look at the bed. He'd been there. They'd made love. Or had she dreamt it? She couldn't be sure. Such was the torture of addiction.

She stepped out the back, cleaned her hands with bottled water. The cuts weren't deep. Superficial. Unlike her broken soul.

The air was calm. The sun was high. Oddly high for being an autumn day.

"Mr. Darci," she called out. A crawling sense he was near made her very uncomfortable. Not that there was any movement or sound to indicate anyone was near. She touched her jaw. The man in her dreams was her father yet the voice had belonged to the caretaker. Had he touched her in the night? Picked her up from the ruin that was another attempt of cowardice? Or was all of it merely a nightmare brought on by a combination of too much to drink and neurosis?

He'd been correct. She couldn't stay here the full two weeks. She couldn't stay here another two hours. Being alone was not the healing opportunity she'd hoped for. It was making her worse. She was defeated. The nightmares, the dreams, all too real.

She'd make a lunch, pack her belongings and go.

But when she tried to open the door to leave it was stuck.

"Promissssse."

She put her suitcase down and tried again, using her shoulder to push while she turned the knob. It wouldn't move, as though a mighty force pushed back at it from the outside. She went to the window to inspect. No one was there.

So she dragged her case to the back door. Farther to walk but she'd manage.

That door was secured shut as well.

"You promised meeeeeee."

She shook her head trying to ignore the voice inside. Her heart raced. She'd just opened the goddamn door minutes earlier to wash her hands over the back step!

"Mr. Darci?" she called out, suspecting the worst. Was he up to some sadistic trick, making her even more fearful, if that was possible? She pounded her fists on the door, screaming like a child who was being punished, locked in her room for being naughty. "Let me out! Right now!"

This was incredulous. What was he doing? Why?

Strangers. Sometimes strangers killed other strangers just for the thrill of it. She backed away from the door, peering out each window to catch a glimpse of her gaoler. The impulse to barricade herself inside became tantamount. She pulled the bed across the front door, braced the table against the back door. It did little to calm her panic. Especially since the windows could be broken. She was a target. Her imagination made her nerves worse.

No one can hear me scream.

Lola decided to hide in the loft, at least until she regained composure. She could do it. She was stronger than all this. She just needed to take a few deep breaths in a place that was safe.

She pulled the rope and scrambled up the stairs. She yanked the stairs up and the square door clicked into place. She sat, cross-legged and listened.

Slowly her pulse calmed but her angst that the caretaker was lurking outside, or even downstairs, remained.

The single window framed a funnel of sunlight. Scattered papers blanketed the floor. She picked up one piece and held it into the light. Frantic words slurred together on the page denoting a sheer torturous hell.

where are you why do you make promises you wont keep why do you keep leaving why cant you hear me call out for you i need your company i need to feel your body next to mine hear your heart beat know i am alive you said you would wait for me be with me always and then i find you with that man on your bed and you leave me to be with him just the same way that other bitch left me and now you do the same youre no better no better youre worse stupid bitch bitch misery misery needs company misery needs company

"Oh my god," Lola whispered. "Daniel, I don't understand."

She picked up another piece of paper.

your fault your fault you don't care she doesnt care i don't either i am dead i am dead and i am lost in this hell without anyone to love me you touched me lola you touched my soul i thought you loved me you said you loved me forever and then you left me alone to rot lola lola lola i am dead because of you and her and lies and you will suffer with me always because i am alone in hell

Every paper scattered across the floor was printed with the ramblings of a madman, Daniel Stone. "I never left," she protested aloud. "I have been here all along. I watched and waited for you. Only you. There's no other man. I waited for you. You left me."

misery misery misery needs company you must stay here forever with me i will not let you leave i will do whatever i have to do to keep you here with me because i love you i need you i love you love you love you i want your company because you are misery as i am misery i am dead and you are dead misery needs company

The typewriter in the corner bounced violently up and down, nonsense typing, meaningless angry frantic pounding. And suddenly it flipped over. The room fell deathly silent.

A squeak from the rafter.

A shadow beneath, dangling lifelessly from a rope.

Black hair curled over the bare tanned shoulders. He wore jeans and work boots, boots mere inches above the kicked over typewriter. His head was twisted to one side. His tongue was swollen, lips black, eyes open, staring blindly into eternity.

She screamed in blinding white horror. One elongated sharp shriek took every bit of air from her lungs. The floor beneath her gave way—the square door had snapped open and she fell, rolling on the stairs, landing with a deafening thud.

Physical pain besieged her and she was unable to move. Except...she opened her eyes. The room glowed with an eerie pallid light. Sitting calmly beside her, cross-legged, in a halo of swaying yellow, was Daniel. His face was fresh, flushed with adoration, his lips parted to an ecstatic smile.

Wind chimes tinkled gently.

She forced a half-smile in return. He stroked her hair, tipping his head to one side, a cascade of black curls sweeping one bare shoulder. The laceration from the hanging was no longer visible. Another bad dream, she mused numbly.

"You have such a nice tan," she said with incredible effort. It hurt to speak.

He took hold of her wrist and squeezed. More pain. She grimaced.

Then he showed her the knife.

"Daniel," she murmured. "I can't hurt any longer. I am too tired."

"I know," he said adamantly. He twisted the blade. It caught the light and temporarily blinded her. He folded forward, brushed her lips with his, teasing her with the flutter of his tongue. "I'll make it all go away. I'll be here for you, on the other side. I promise to be here for you always. I'll make your hurt all go away."

"I knew you would. That's why I came here. To find peace. To find you."

He laughed. It sounded like wind chimes.

"Ready?" he asked, his voice light, cheerful.

"Ready."

He took a hold of her wrist, kissed her palm then casually sliced skin, tendons, veins, effortlessly and unemotionally. She watched his face, an unwavering expression, and felt nothing except a slight, warm trickle down her fingers. He took her other wrist. Another quick slice.

He smiled. "I'll be here waiting. I promise." He put the knife gently on the floor. His eyes narrowed and he leaned back to watch. And wait.

She smiled back. Her eyes felt heavy.

The walls fell away. The sun was high in the sky for an autumn day.

She took a long deep breath. The air was sweet. Water lapped against the shore. The leaves fluttered in the dying breeze. She wanted to sketch a picture of the serenity but her hands were far too limp. She bled, a flow of warmth from inside she hadn't known was there. And as her senses dulled, he reached over and held her against his solid tanned chest.

* * * *

"How long you reckon on staying, buddy?"

"Two, maybe three weeks." Spike pulled his guitar out from the back seat and leaned it against his car. "I'm going to write a shit load of songs. New best selling album in the works." He grinned. "I'm the comeback kid."

"Yeah, ya think?"

"I know so. Rehab works wonders for the fallen. I am a new man."

The caretaker leaned against his rusty half ton, stuck a hand rolled cigarette between his knife thin lips, cupping the match so that the stiff wind off the melting ice won't kill the flame. He sucked the cigarette hard, blowing smoke out his mouth directly into the musician's face. It evaporated within seconds. "I highly fucking doubt it."

He stood there, staring at Spike with black sunken eyes. The musician was taken aback. He had met some twisted assholes in his life and this old timer was right up there with the worst of them. Creepy even. Something about those eyes. Like they were dead, or... "Fine thing to say. But I don't give a damn. Just give me the keys and piss off."

The caretaker smirked.

Those beady eyes shifted sideways to the cabin. Then back. His mouth pinched a harder grin. He thrust his hand in his jeans pocket and passed over a key. When Spike reached out to take it he took hold of his wrist. He wrenched it so violently the musician dropped to his knees with a short sharp holler.

The caretaker folded forward. His breath stunk of nicotine. Intermingled with it was a whiff of whiskey. "Don't touch the sketches or the typewriter," he growled, barely moving his lips. He hadn't blinked. "The former owners wouldn't like it. Don't say you ain't been warned. Buddy."

He let go of the wrist, wrenched open the door to his truck, and hopped behind the wheel. The window was down. He shifted the gears. The truck slowly rolled backwards. "Bottle of Jack in the fridge," he said, the cigarette hanging out one side of his mouth. "You'll need it."

Spike flipped the old man his middle finger. "Crazy ass," he muttered. Still, he was left with an unsettling feeling. Sketches? Typewriter? They couldn't have been valuable possessions if they were left behind. He chuckled, plotting to destroy both, just to piss off the miserable old caretaker.

But before he could proceed with his plot, a woman's playful laughter caught his attention. Spike scanned the cabin's front porch where he thought the sound had originated. Then the yard. He didn't see a thing. "Hello?" he called out. Another giggle carried on the breeze.

"Well, well, sweetheart. Show yourself and if you're a lucky girl you might get a bit of Spike tonight." He strummed his crotch as though it was a guitar.

Then his blood ran cold.

Two figures appeared from the cabin. A man, black hair swaying over bare shoulders, wearing jeans and boots stepped off the porch. The woman by his side laughed, spun playfully around and threw her arms around his waist. They kissed, their bodies swaying together. Light glowed around them, glowed and then shivered, bathing them in an eerie hue.

Spike squinted harder. "Holy shit!" he muttered. Both figures were transparent, the edges of their bodies dissolving, reappearing, pulsating with the shimmering light that held them together. And both stopped, aware of an intruder, turning to glare directly to where Spike stood.

He reached blindly for the car door, not even blinking for fear the ghostly figures might attack. He trembled violently, barely able to get the keys into the ignition. The car spun in reverse and was gone.

A woman's rapturous laughter erupted and finally faded.

And wind chimes tinkled in the ice cold breeze before falling forever silent.

CONFESSIONS OF
A NYMPHO

Ashley Ladd

Dedication

To Clark Kent, Indiana Jones, Rick O'Connell, Johnny
Castle, Captain Jack Sparrow, Will Turner, Hans Solo,
Rhett Butler, Mr. Darcy, Cliff Secord (Rocketeer),
Captain Kirk, Commander Will Ryker, Jack T. Colton
and all the yummy romantic heroes
that worship me in my dreams.

Chapter One

Wantonly squirming in her chair, Tatiana Reece viewed the erotic photos of naked big busted women riding the juiciest, most engorged cocks she'd ever seen. They were meatier than any of the ones she'd found in her older brother's erotica when they'd been kids. Feeling like a cat in heat, she sensually rubbed her pussy back and forth against the buttery leather seat. Leaning back, she reached inside the gaping bodice of her filmy teddy, pinched her budding nipples, then rolled them between her fingers. After shivers of delight raced down her spine and the earth quaked, she typed the sensation into her new blog, 'Confessions of a Nympho'.

Our gazes locked across the crowded, smoky club and my heart stopped... I couldn't breathe. He was so perfect — gorgeous, tanned, and so deliciously muscular — even the gods would be jealous. He was the clichéd tall, dark, and ruggedly handsome. Just the way I lusted after them. Who cared if the guy possessed a brain or personality? I only cared how wonderful he'd make me feel for the night since I doubted I'd ever see him again. I longed to gorge myself on hot, wet, wild sex until dawn.

My blood sizzling, I licked my lips in slow, deliberate invitation. Not waiting for him to make the first move, I went on the prowl, sashaying boldly up to him and gazing deeply into his deep brown eyes.

My gaze lingered on his luscious chiselled lips before I let it drop to his firm, outthrust chin, and then lower still until it caressed the inviting bulge in his sinfully tight jeans. A predator, I sat on his lap and curled my arm around his neck as I slid against his hard length.

"Hi handsome," I drawled as I pressed my breasts against his warm chest. "Are you looking for some company?"

Passion eclipsed the shock in his eyes, and he winked at me. "Hello to you, too." He took my hand and put it on his delicious bulge as he nuzzled my neck.

God, but his lips felt sensational as they feathered kisses down the arch of my neck and then nuzzled my shoulder, primitively erotic, driving up my fever.

"Let's go somewhere more—*private*." I'd almost said my place but didn't want him hanging around if he turned out to be a serial killer or a stalker like my ex. The second scared me more since I'm a second degree black belt in Taekwondo and I can take care of myself. To punctuate my special request, I unbuttoned his jeans and slid my hand inside his pants. Finding his feverish cock, and I curled my fingers around it and began to pump the thick, heated shaft. Rock hard and huge, it throbbed just for me. I creamed my panties as I leaned closer and stuck my tongue down his throat.

Caught in a web of delightful lust, my heart hammering against my ribs, my thighs quivering, my mind in a heady haze, I'm not quite sure how we got out the door. In a tangle of arms and legs and tongues, I'm sure. The next thing I knew, we were kissing, caressing, and practically having sex on the street as we dragged each other to the nearest hotel. I can't even tell you the name. All I cared about was the king-size soft bed and clean sheets. And it was ours until noon — a lifetime…an infinitesimal moment frozen in time.

We tore off each other's clothes as we stumbled across the threshold and they puddled at our feet. Mr. Wonderful ripped my blouse to shreds, but hell if I cared. I yanked his jeans down to his knees and took his underwear prisoner in my teeth and dragged them down.

Begging me to take a taste, his cock sprung out. Milky droplets of his seed clung to the end of the velvety red head of his shaft so I stuck out my tongue and caught a drop. His flesh seared mine, and yearning to feel the satiny flesh against my lips, I leaned closer. When I opened my lips wider to take the head into my mouth, he pushed his staff deep into my throat.

The curly hair on his legs tickled my face and my bare breasts. The door slammed and only then did I wonder if anyone had seen us, but that only enflamed my desire. Little had I realised I was a voyeuristic until that moment, but I'm not exactly shocked. I mean, I write erotic romance. I kiss and tell. Right?

Then I wrapped my hand around his cock and pumped in rhythm to his raspy moans. I felt headier than I've ever felt before. I'd never exuded such power over any man but I loved it.

He fucked my mouth with a fervour that left me breathless. Greedy for more, I clamped his firm buttocks in my palms and held him captive. I tried to pull back for air, but he tangled his fingers in my hair and held me tight. He pressed my head deeper against his groin and ground his cock into me.

Ravenous, I lost myself in Mr. Tall, Dark and Luscious. I ran the tip of my tongue across the slit of his cock, coaxing his seed which I craved more than any decadently rich chocolate or ambrosia.

He rammed his cock to the back of my throat again. And again.

When his seed burst forth, I gulped down the creamiest, tastiest come in the world. Unable to get my fill, I sucked harder like a greedy little bitch.

Finally, he dragged me against his chest. He ravaged my lips then scooped me into his arms and laid me gently on the bed.

On fire, I opened my arms wide and welcomed him against my heart. He captured my lips and crushed me to him as his cock grazed my thighs, swelling larger with every beat of his hammering heart.

My pussy throbbing, I spread my legs wide. His thumb massaged my clit until I moaned in ecstasy against his lips. I ground against his hand as he thrust his finger into my well with more and more fervour. Nympho that I am, I yearned for his big cock.

"Fuck my brains out," I begged, breathless. I'd never wanted anything more in my life.

With a primitive growl from deep in his soul, he yanked his hand away and drove his cock into me with a force that stole my breath. "Anything you want, baby." He buried himself into me so deeply our souls united. He pumped with savage fierceness.

I love it when men call me "babe" or "baby". I find that so utterly sexy. Maybe it's because my ex thought he was being romantic if he remembered my name rather than "hey you".

Mr. Luscious sucked and nipped and teased me unmercifully. To my shock, and to my utter delight, he spanked me! Not just a little slap and tickle, but a hard, stinging smack on my bum. Then, as my flesh was still raw and ultra-sensitised, he cooled it with long sweeps of his tongue. Only I didn't stay cool long, not long at all. Within seconds, a wildfire swept me away and as Mr. Luscious drove into me one final, earth-shattering time, stars burst in my heaven. Quivering, murmuring my name against his lips as if I was the most precious thing in his universe, he cradled me against his heart.

Unsatiated, thirsting for more, I grappled him onto his back. I swung my leg across his girth and I pinned his wrists to the mattress. Inch by excruciating inch, our juices mingled as I slid down his succulent crimson cock until I sheathed his entire length. It seemed that my Taekwondo training was coming in handy for something other than self-defence, not that it had scared away my crazy ex.

"You're so hot, baby," I murmured as I dropped kisses along his jaw and down the column of his long throat to his impressive chest.

"Nimble minx." His hips thrust in perfect rhythm with mine as we enjoyed the dance.

I was impressed that he could keep up with me as I have more energy than any mere male I'd met. *Maybe I would ask his name if I still liked him in the morning...*

The timer shrilled and Tatiana jumped, nearly toppling over in her chair she was so startled. She glared at the lousy alarm clock, angry that it had jarred her out of her sexy dreams. "Damn! It can't be time yet, can it?" She had to meet with her accountant in an hour. Of all the unsexy things to interrupt.

She sprinted upstairs to the shower and sluiced off her musky odour. As she towel dried, she spoke to herself in the mirror as was her habit. "I couldn't show up in Vogt's office smelling of sex, could I? He'd so tell mom and she'd harp on me forevermore." The staid old accountant had been friends with her family forever and would be sure to report any state of dishabille.

She ran a comb through her damp hair, donned the first pair of slacks she could find—ripped jeans—and tucked an old T-shirt into the high waistband. Her garb wasn't even in the same league as her fantasy clothes in her blog story, but who cared? All she cared was that she was clean and didn't smell as if she'd just rolled out of a night of debauchery.

Grimacing at the clock on the wall, she spread a little foundation across her cheeks to hide the sea of freckles she so detested, dabbed on a bit of lip gloss, and sifted some mascara over her too-light lashes. Then she crammed all her year's receipts into a couple boxes and her purse, and ran out the door. It wouldn't do to be late again. He'd threatened to drop her flat on her ass if she didn't learn how to stay on schedule. The man was a stickler for being on time. Unlike anyone else she knew, he'd even been born precisely on his due date. "He's gonna kill me."

* * * *

Horace "Ace" Dyer poured over his accounting ledgers. He couldn't keep from glancing at his watch wondering when *she* would cross the threshold of his office. *She*, of course, was the famous romance novelist, Tatiana Reece, and he'd been in love with her since the first time they'd met two years before during the tax season from hell.

Well, they hadn't exactly met. When last she'd visited the office, he'd been only a junior accountant on staff, and thus he'd only seen her from afar. He'd been assigned to do her receivables, and he'd been smitten with the siren ever since.

To think he'd almost stayed in the Army instead of getting out and becoming an accountant.

Late, a literal mess with receipts crammed into her purse, a shoebox, and even the pockets of her ripped jeans, she'd run into his boss's office. Her books had been totally out of whack and if it had been anybody else but the raven-haired nymph, he was sure the old goat would have bid her goodbye. But she was the daughter of his best buddy, practically his own daughter he'd said, so he'd let it go with a warning.

One glowing smile from Tatiana Reece's glossy lips, one devilish wink from her mischievous eyes, and Ace had been a goner. She'd stolen his heart and bewitched him.

Unfortunately, the minx hadn't noticed he was alive. He might as well have been a fly on the wall. Oh, she was polite and kind to everyone, not the diva he'd expected. But she'd rushed in and out as if she'd barely saw him, like he was an ATM on the wall, just a piece of the scenery in his boss's office.

He didn't like being scenery.

He'd heard she'd broken up with her boyfriend and he'd fantasised that maybe she'd notice him this year. He wasn't the lackey he used to be. Now he was an up-and-coming accountant in the firm. Partnership glistened in his future.

Still, she'd probably never notice him in the background again. At most she might view him as a boring accountant in an asexual blue suit and tie with wingtipped shoes and tortoise shell glasses. He was completely, disgustingly organised down to arranging his pens in order of size, while she was a delightful jumble of colour and life.

Unable to help himself, he counted the seconds until her arrival, almost squirming in his big leather chair. This year, his boss had come down with a last minute stomach bug and had left Ace in charge. He was ready for her, even if he was quaking in his wingtips. He'd cleared a few days in his calendar for her job, and he'd cleared his desk in the fathomless hope of ravaging her on it.

Shovelling his fingers through his neatly combed hair, he chuckled mirthlessly at his hopeless fantasies. What would a luscious, infamous siren like Tatiana ever see in him? He was geekier than Clark Kent and Peter Parker rolled into one. She lived in a world beyond the stratosphere with steroid-induced male cover models that would put Hercules to shame.

Finally, twenty-six minutes after her scheduled time, he heard the squeal of brakes and then a slammed door. Unable to help himself, he wandered to the window and gazed upon his fantasy woman as she dropped her purse, sent several pieces of paper aflutter across the newly paved parking lot, and groped for them on her hands and knees. Although he fervently hoped that no crucial receipts blew away, he didn't bemoan the view of her curvy tush sticking up in the air, going up and down as she crawled about. He blessed the modern wonders of tinted glass that enabled him to ogle her undetected. He supposed if he was a true gentleman, a real hero, he'd run down there and help her gather her stuff. But the view and the fantasies were just too erotic. Besides, he didn't want to get caught watching her. She'd know he'd been spying on her if he rushed to her aid.

Finally, she managed to snag the last receipt and stuff it into her purse and wrangle shut the jammed holder. Then, as if she sensed his perusal, she gazed up at his window.

His heart racing, he jumped back, all the while telling himself he was all kinds of stupid. But just in case the tinted glass wasn't as effective — or just in case she possessed x-ray vision — he didn't want to be caught. Too late, probably, if she could see through the glass.

He settled back into his seat, took out his ledger and favourite gold pen and pretended to be engrossed in his books. When she knocked at his open door, he pretended to be startled, not a far jump as his heart almost pounded through his ribs.

"Knock, knock. Sorry I'm late. Are you Horace Dyer? The secretary told me you're filling in for Mr. Vogt." Tatiana's form cast a shadow to the corner of Ace's desk and then she traipsed across the carpeted floor without invitation. A frown marred her beautiful face.

He squirmed at her nearness and the sense of intimacy she evoked. Then he grimaced. "Please call me 'Ace'. No one calls me 'Horace'."

She dropped her bag and boxes onto his desk and then plopped into the chair facing him. Crossing her never-ending model-like legs, she dangled them in front of him.

Fixated as he was on her beautifully manicured, sexy-as-hell airbrushed toes and the slim ankle decorated with a classy silver chain, he could hardly breathe. With every cell in his overheated being, he dragged his focus back to her face then gulped again. Those incredible eyes were pinpointed on him, punctuated with long, lush, dark lashes.

"Earth to Ace," she drawled huskily. Leaning forward she snapped her fingers in front of his nose. Then she waved cheerily, her delicious perfume wafting from her wrists.

Dizzy from her scent, Ace pulled back and forced a professional smile to his lips. "Hello." He kicked himself for sounding like he had a stick poked up his ass. Why did this woman turn him to mush? Or rather into the biggest geek on the planet?

She frowned and stared at the pink watch on her wrist. "You are expecting me now, aren't you? Did I get the days mixed up again?" She began to fish through her purse.

When she started to extract her date book, he waved it away, and found his voice. "Y-yes." He had to clear the damned frog from his throat and wished he could roll back the clock and start this session over. Hell, he wished he could begin their entire relationship over. "I've been expecting you. What have you got for me?" How he wished it was herself, her hot, supple body and all her love and eternal devotion.

She tapped a long airbrushed nail that matched her toes on the box closest to her. "The usual stuff I have for Mr. Vogt. All my business receipts." She leaned closer, licked her glossy lips, and smiled conspiratorially. "I hope you can find me a lot of *big* deductions this year."

He swallowed hard. He had something *big* for her all right, but it was inside his pants, swelling larger with every second. Embarrassed, he slid further under the desk to hide his source of discomfort.

"We'll see," he said noncommittally, without any hint of emotion. "I'll do my best." He kicked himself for getting shy, not at all like the kick-ass romance heroes she lived for. How could he ever win a woman like her by acting like this?

She dumped the contents of both boxes onto his desk and sifted through them. "I went to several conferences this year and bought a new computer. Those hotel rooms are downright outrageous!"

Hotel rooms? He gulped. How he'd like to share a hotel room with her. He wondered if she went alone and took the receipt from her hand. When her fingers grazed his, shivers raced down his spine. Unable to stop himself, he asked, "Is this for single or double occupancy?"

She snatched the receipt from him, grazing his knuckles again. "Let me see. I get a roommate whenever I can, but a few times I went alone."

His jealousy surged and he longed to ask the roommate's name. Some of those nearly naked Tarzan-type cover models pictured with her all over the romance magazines? Not that he'd ever admit to reading those or keeping track of her doings. He'd sooner cut out his tongue.

"How many? Conferences, I mean? Help me sort these into categories." Or else they'd be there all night. On retrospect that might not be a bad idea…

She squinted at a computer printout in her hand. "What about websites? Aren't they tax deductible?"

Loosening the tie that threatened to choke him, he nodded and tried to keep his voice steady. "Yes, of course."

She leaned further forward and gazed deeply into his eyes. Her ample breasts strained against her T-shirt. The nipples budded against the flimsy cotton. "I mean, if I have more than one website? I just opened this new one, plus I have pages on some romance writers' group pages."

When he took the receipt from her outstretched fingers, her flowery writing on the back caught his eye, and he flipped it over. Reading it, his heart skipped several beats. *Confessions of a Nympho* blog. It contained the website url, and he memorised it. Like he could forget a name like that? It was burned into his consciousness.

Confessions of a Nympho? His cock throbbed almost ripping open his zipper. His blood sizzled. He couldn't wait to visit her blog and read her deepest, darkest fantasies. Or were they fantasies? Did she act them out? Was she really a nymphomaniac?

He went on autopilot for the rest of their session. All he could think about was making love to the exquisite nymph until she forgot every other man who'd ever existed. If it took every second of every day to satisfy her, so be it. He'd make the sacrifice...

* * * *

Thrilled that her new accountant had promised a ton of terrific tax deductions, Tatiana tunelessly sang at the top of her lungs to her favourite songs all the way home from his office. She couldn't care less that she sang off-key. She was already an American Idol, just in a non-vocal venue. She laughed at her moment of conceitedness. Well, she hoped to be famous and loved. The fact that she still owed a lot of moula to Uncle Sam despite the huge deductions Ace had found, attested to the fact that her career was going well. She had no complaints. Career-wise, that was...

If only her love life would grow half as exciting as her fantasised blog adventures.

Since her break-up with the jerk last year, it had been a barren wasteland without an attractive man in sight. She found it downright hilarious that her readers presumed she had the most romantic life in the world or at least, the best sex in town. No way could she admit to being such a failure. They'd probably tar and feather her. Worse, they'd never buy another book.

Sex? What was sex? Words on paper. An elusive desire. Lies in a blog. Promotion and money.

God, but she was a *whore*! She sold sex!

Mirth bubbled up in her at the visualisation of the new guy's totally red face when he'd read the words *Confession of a Nympho* on her receipt. She'd girded herself to do the Heimlich manoeuvre on the man.

He was kind of cute, in a preppy but geeky sort of way. She wondered if he ever took off those horn-rimmed glasses? Maybe during sex? He looked as if he'd only engage in completely vanilla, missionary sex. He was probably still a virgin.

Giggles overwhelmed her when she tried to envision the straight-laced man having doggy-style sex, or more hilarious yet, a threesome.

"Oh, you're so bad, girl!" Mentally, she slapped herself for being so cruel to the new guy. "He's good looking—in an anal sort of way." He might actually be pretty exciting if he didn't slick back his dark hair, lost the glasses and the outdated monkey suit as well as his whole rigid demeanour.

An idiot in a Mercedes cut her off, almost pushing her off the road into a canal, and cursing loudly, she slammed on her brakes. Her thoughts turned to promoting her books and her latest promotions, specifically her new blog *Confessions of a Nympho*.

On her way home, she took a detour to the big city half an hour away where no one knew her family, stopped at the adult video store and picked up several new X-rated movies. She wondered what Ace would think if he saw her in here with these naughty movies.

Snorting aloud, she drew several curious gazes from the other patrons. Her flesh crawling, she hurried to check out with her selections. Although she needed to practice some hot sex, if only for her book's sake, none of these slimy characters were remotely acceptable. It looked as if fantasy would have to do for another night.

Finally at home, she slipped into her room and slid a porno flick into her DVD player. Feeling guiltily decadent, she exchanged the white cotton sheets on her bed for a new red satin set that had just arrived in the mail and spread out across them. They felt so slick, so cool against her flesh, she rolled around like a cat in heat. Well, wasn't she?

As the couples on screen licked and kissed and fucked, she pleasured herself with the new dildo that had also arrived in the mail. God but it was huge, stretching her, going in and out. If only there was a warm body with a hot tongue, strong arms to hold her, and a swiftly beating heart to lay her ear against.

And if horses could fly...

She pretended her fantasy man, Mr. Luscious, was ravaging her, losing his heart and soul to her, and finally, with the long shaft rammed up her pussy, she came.

Her hot, milky liquid poured out of her pussy, spilling onto her new sheets. Writhing and moaning, she wriggled the make-believe cock inside her, stretching her insides. Her thumb caressed her clit until she came again, screaming in ecstasy.

But how much better would it be to have a real, flesh-and-blood man in her bed, covering her, loving her, worshipping her? And for her to worship?

She craved love and romance, not mere sex. With a sudden burst of anger, she hurled the dildo at the far wall. Then she clasped her arms across her heaving chest and stared at the mark it left on her wallpaper.

"Okay," she murmured as she stared at the writhing couples having an orgy on screen. "It's time to take my love life into my own hands." At the very least, she'd have a *real* sex life. No more of this fantasy bullshit or fake, plastic cocks.

At least not exclusively.

She washed up, changed the sheets again, and then went downstairs to her computer. Grimacing, she muttered, "Promotion time. Gotta pay the bills." That electric company was getting downright greedy.

Promotion was the bane of her life. Why couldn't she just do what she loved? Write! Why did she have to worry about this promotion bullshit? Someday, she hoped she'd have to pay Uncle Sam a *lot* more and be able to hire a publicist to do all her promotion and that would be the glorious day she could spend all her time writing.

Until then... She opened her new blog and started to type.

He asked if a friend could join us tonight...

Hornier than I'd ever been, I quipped "Sure! The more the merrier!" even as I squirmed wantonly, practically coming right then and there. I was so turned on I was ready to fuck him in the middle of the highway, in front of everyone. I reached over, unzipped his slacks, drew out his swelling cock and dipped my head onto his lap.

When I licked the head of his velvety shaft, the car swerved, and he swore.

"Do you want me to stop?" I asked slyly, knowing the answer.

"Never. But give a guy some warning."

I had when I'd released his cock, hadn't I? *Sheesh!*

He pushed my shirt off my shoulder and started kneading my nipples, making me squirm. So I took his beautiful shaft deeper into my mouth. Then I slid my mouth up and down as I held his balls in my hands.

He pulled off the side of the road and cut the engines. "We're going to wreck if you keep that up, baby."

With his cock still in my mouth, moist and slick, his cum all over my lips, I smiled up at him. "That good?"

He nodded as he clamped my head securely against his feverish groin. "That good. Only one thing better," he drawled.

I could think of one. Or two. His hot, dangerous cock fucking me. Better yet, two hot, dangerous cocks fucking me, making me beg for mercy.

Screaming and quaking, I came. I didn't just come, I flowed like a river.

"Where's your friend? *Let's go get him...*"

An instant message popped onto the screen and Tatiana jumped back so fast her chair almost toppled. It swayed precariously, rocked, and skid on the floor pad. When she righted herself, her heart hammered so hard she almost hyperventilated. Clutching her throat, she inched back to the screen and cautiously read the message.

"Hey, babe. Are you *really* a nympho?"

Chapter Two

Tatiana reread the IM a dozen times then poised her fingers over her keyboard. Her fingers tapped tinnily on the keys. "Do I answer him? Or do I block him?" She looked at the screen name again—Act1.

"Why do you think I'm a nympho?" she finally keyed even as her heart continued racing. Aloud, she muttered in a shaky voice, "Am I really doing this?"

Doing what?

Hell! She had no idea what she was doing. Or what she was about to do.

Yet didn't she want to take her love life in her own hands?

Closing her eyes, she jabbed the send key. She had to start somewhere. Fingering her imaginary black belt, she hoped she wasn't ten kinds of an idiot.

Opening her eyes slowly, she peered at the screen.

"Your blog…*Confessions of a Nympho*…unless it's all a lie… Is it?"

She gulped. It wasn't so much a lie as it was an act—an act in the name of promotion. Or was it all for promotion of her books? For that matter, her books could be considered lies, too. She didn't write about her own sex life.

She shook her head. No, it wasn't all about promotion of her books. She was horny, extremely horny. She hadn't been laid in more than two years and she wasn't ready to go steady with that danged dildo. Inhaling deeply, she typed, "It's not a lie. Do you want a sample? Are you brave enough?"

She almost choked. "Did I really just say that?" she yelped, making her cat scamper away from his cosy perch on the computer desk. She almost collapsed the IM and the entire Internet connection.

"Just say where and when. I'll be there."

The cogs in her mind whirling, she stared at the black typeface for several moments. Finally, holding her breath, she tapped out, "How do you know if you live near me? I could be on the other side of the world."

"Then I'll hop on a plane. I want you. You're so hot."

That hot? Hot enough to jump on a jet plane? Desperate, maybe?

"Tell me where you want to meet. And when." The IM seemed to pulse in front of her eyes.

"Before I say yes, tell me why I should meet you." She swiped away the perspiration beading on her brow, then she scuttled into the kitchen, grabbed a cold bottle of water and took a swig. She ran the cool bottle across her forehead then held it between her breasts. God, but she was about to burst into flames. Was she actually thinking about doing this?

"Get a grip," she murmured to herself as she ambled back to her computer, about ready to strip off her stifling clothes she was still so very hot.

"I'm tall, dark, and handsome, just the way you like." Her eyes widened and she stared at the words. Her heart stopped for an infinitesimal moment. "How do you know that?"

"You said so. In your blog."

Duh. Her lungs opened and she took in a breath.

"How old are you?" She prayed he wouldn't be too young or too old. Seven years in one direction or the other was her limit. Sometimes ten years older, but never ten years younger. Twenty-one year olds, even twenty-two year olds, were normally much too immature for her liking.

"Does age matter? As long as I'm not under eighteen?"

Before she could email back, he replied, "I don't rob cradles... I'm thirty-four. Single. Never been married. Not in a committed relationship. Caucasian. I earn a good living. No kids except for one usually behaved collie. I'm 6'3", have dark hair, and I weigh 184. I'm athletic and in shape. Satisfied?"

Satisfied? Hell, she was panting to meet this Mr. Perfect. *If he was on the level...*

Only one way to find out... Quivering so much as to start an earthquake, she typed, "Okay. Meet me at the Hilton in Ft. Lauderdale this Saturday night at seven pm."

What seemed like only half a second later he answered, "Which one? There are several."

"The one in Deerfield Beach, off I-95." She thought about some of her favourite romantic movies. "I have long, dark, curly hair just past my shoulders, am about 5'8", and I'll be wearing..." Um, what should she wear for such a momentous, decadent occasion? She thought hard, and then smiled. "A tan raincoat with a see-through teddy beneath." She'd be so arrested if she got pulled over by a cop. But that thought just catapulted her already soaring temperature.

"Baby, I can't wait. How about tonight?"

Tonight! She spluttered the water in her mouth all over her computer screen. Angry at herself, she retrieved a paper towel and cleaned it off.

"Tonight? You live here? In Ft. Lauderdale?"

"Round abouts. How about nine pm?"

"Tonight? nine pm?" she echoed, feeling dumber than dumb. This was surreal. She pinched herself to make sure she wasn't dreaming, and she yelped when it hurt. "You really live here?"

Her flesh tingled anew and her juices flowed fast and furious. Was she really going to get fucked tonight? For real? She was going to be held in real arms, against a real chest, and she was actually going to be kissed long and slow and sensually?

"I just booked room 219 for us and some champagne on ice. You like?"

Her eyes almost bulged out of their sockets. Her heart slammed against her chest. Scared to death, yet totally turned on, she clamped down on her fears. She reminded herself that she was a second degree black belt and she could defend herself, otherwise, she'd never dream of meeting a stranger in a hotel room for some anonymous sex. "I *love* it. Nine pm it is."

Before she could change her mind, she closed the IM. Barely able to gulp in air, she went to her sink, bent over it and poured the rest of the bottled water over her head. "You're crazy, girl!"

* * * *

Ace paced the room, wondering what Tatiana would say when she discovered he was her illicit rendezvous?

He'd dimmed the lights, lit about a hundred candles, and ditched his glasses in favour of contacts. He'd stopped by the barber shop for a new haircut, a dry style, so that his hair was no longer slicked back away from his face. His forehead itched where a lock insisted on curling down, but he liked the look of it in the mirror so refrained from messing with it. He'd also left the stuffy suit at home in favour of laid back jeans and a soft T-shirt that emphasised his muscles. He was a new man, *her* man, for at least the night. However, he intended to make this last much longer than a night if he could. He hoped it would multiply into a lifetime.

As usual, the clock ticked past nine pm with no Tatiana in sight. Hoping to catch a glimpse of her in her raincoat, hoping she hadn't had second thoughts, he glanced out the window. The promised teddy made him hard and he peeled the T-shirt and jeans off and stepped into the silk shorts he'd bought just for this special occasion.

Ten minutes passed then twenty. Finally, at half past the hour, a loud knock rapped on the door, and he expelled a long, held breath. Gathering his wits, squaring his shoulders, and raking his shaky fingers through his hair, he crossed the room and put his hand on the doorknob. Then he paused, hoping that Tatiana wouldn't reject him. Or worse, laugh at him.

The knock sounded again, less sure this time. Sucking in a long breath, knowing this was his moment of truth, he turned the knob and opened the door wide enough to peer outside. He didn't want some maid or someone with the wrong room number to scream about an undressed pervert. When he spied the beautiful Tatiana smiling up at him in the promised raincoat, his heart raced.

"Hi…Act1, right? I don't even know your name," the siren crooned as she pushed the door wider and sashayed into the room past him.

Stunned and insulted that she didn't recognise him, he swallowed his pride, as he nodded. He wondered if this is how Clark Kent felt every time Lois Lane stared through him.

Huskily, his nerves wildly zinging, he forced himself out of his shyness, and became the self-confident, take-charge man she waxed on about in her naughty blog, throughout her many romantic novels, the one he'd been in his Army days. "Tonight is about your fantasies. Call me whatever you like."

A saucy smile curved her lips and she stepped closer. Her fingers played with the buttons of her coat but didn't release them. "You've been reading my blog. I'll just call you 'Mr. Wonderful'. Is that okay?"

Mr. Wonderful? He liked the sound of that so he nodded.

Closing the gap between them, he towered over her and leaned slightly towards her. "That's me. What's your name?"

She licked her lips with the tip of her tongue and winked up at him. "Tati."

Naughty Tati. He liked it. It definitely suited her tonight.

He allowed himself to touch her magnificent hair, the hair he'd dreamed about touching. The red highlights in her hair glowed under the moonlight streaming in through the blinds. He sniffed and drank in her essence. "You're gorgeous, Tati. I'm the luckiest man in the world that you've chosen me tonight."

When her gaze became dazed, he congratulated himself on putting that exquisite look on her face. He dropped feathery kisses to her perfumed flesh. Like jasmine, she smelled heavenly. "You must be hot in that raincoat."

She quivered against his lips and closed her eyes. Her long, black lashes made a demure fan against her high cheekbones and he dropped kisses on each one.

"Absolutely sweltering."

"So take it off." He couldn't wait to see those curves he'd dreamed about kissing and licking and suckling for so long. He spread his palms on the lapels of her jacket and let them slide down to the top buttons. "May I?"

Her splendid eyes darkened and she nodded. "Be my guest."

As he undid the buttons, she leaned forward and kissed his chest. Blazing fire alarms threatened to set off the China syndrome. Her magic wrapped around him as her warm lips continued to caress his bare chest. When her tongue swirled over his nipple, he quivered and pushed her coat off her shoulders.

"You're beautiful," she said in awe as she blazed a trail of kisses to his other nipple.

His heart swelled as his cock flexed. He longed to rub it against her, to release it to her charms. "So are you. Why is it that no one has claimed you for his own?"

Challenge in her eyes, she glanced up at him coyly. "How do you know he hasn't?"

Oh oh. He was revealing too much. Suddenly, he didn't want her to recognise him just yet. He wanted her to be his for as long as he could captivate her. He'd make her fall in love with him before revealing his true identity. Thinking fast, he came up with an answer. Lifting her left hand and caressing her ringless fourth finger, he said huskily, "You wear no man's ring. And you're here with me instead of home with some other lucky guy."

She gazed upon her hand. "I could have taken it off."

He rubbed the smooth finger. "There's no tan line."

She made a moue with her lips. "Maybe I don't expose my skin to the sun's harmful rays."

He gathered her against his chest and rubbed his feverish cock against her pussy. "Ah, so are you cheating with me on some poor guy?" Intoxicated by her luscious scent, he buried his nose in her fragranced hair. "I hope not. I mean, I hope you don't have someone else."

She rubbed against him wantonly but let her gaze slide away from him. With a hesitancy and a catch in her voice, she asked, "Would it matter? This is a one-night fling. You've read my blog. You know my MO."

Not if he could help it. He heard her brave, big words, but he no longer believed them despite tonight's wantonness. She was feeling the chemistry. Finally! Hallelujah!

Unwilling to scare her away, secure in the knowledge that no one had laid claim to her heart, he lied, "No, it doesn't matter. As long as you're mine tonight."

"*All yours.*" She pushed his drawers down his thighs exposing his cock then curled her fingers around its length.

Blood throbbing through it, his hungry cock furiously pulsed. Yearning to know the moist tightness of her, it strained against her. He thrust his hips against her, sliding his hard cock between her legs and moaning when she squeezed her legs tightly about him. Eager to know her more intimately and become one with his lady, he scooped her into his arms and cradled her against his heart.

She curled her arms around his neck, swung her legs gently at his sides and nuzzled her lips against his heart. In a husky voice she drawled, "You're a caveman."

Smiling, he growled just for her as he plundered her lips and drank deeply of her. Hypnotised more than he could have ever dreamed, his tongue mated with hers in the ancient dance. His cock longed to perform a riotous salsa and so he laid her reverently on the large bed.

Before joining her, he peeled off her diaphanous teddy. She lifted her shoulders from the bed as he pulled the top over her arms. She thrust her hips up while he stripped the tiny panties away from her wiry curls. Bewitching him, her musky scent wafted up.

"Have you really done this before?" he couldn't help himself from asking.

She frowned, her thrusting hips coming to a halt midair, just short of his waiting cock. "Made love?"

"Met strangers in hotel rooms?" Wrangling with his jealousy, he wanted to kick himself. He was one inch from paradise and if he drove her away now, he'd never forgive himself.

Shock flashed across her passion-glazed eyes before it was quickly masked. She murmured, "But of course. You've read my blog."

"Of course," he repeated numbly. At least he hadn't driven her away. He decided to lose himself in the night and let fate take things from here as he buried his cock and his heart deep inside her.

Conflicted with raw emotions, Tatiana opened herself to her lover. This man was not only everything she'd ever dreamed of in a man, but so much more. Not only was he handsome, sexy and strong but sweet and tender. His eyes glowed with a rapt intensity that filled the void in her soul. They cherished her as no other pair of eyes had ever done.

But no! It couldn't be love. They'd just met.

So why was her heart singing? It was practically conducting an opera!

The only thing keeping her from totally opening up to this glorious man was his strange questions. Just as she was drowning in him, he'd open his mouth and say something to pull her from her exquisite dream.

She sifted her fingers through his soft, wavy hair, hair so dark it almost gleamed blue. His eyes were such a deep, dark ebony she could happily drown in them, but it was the love and kindness and devotion in them that so mesmerised her.

Strong and chiselled yet warm and oh-so-soft, his lips delighted her. She could feast on him forever and never starve. Again, she parted her lips and pressed them to his. Delving her tongue inside, she invited him to tango with her. When she came up for air, she murmured against his lips, "Why aren't you taken?"

He pulled back a fraction of an inch and then hesitated. Finally, as she clung to his every word, he said, "Because I'm invisible to the woman of my dreams."

Shocked and dismayed on several levels, Tatiana gasped. She ground her hips harder against his, straining to be closer. "How can any woman be so blind?" Yet, she was ever so glad that her competition hadn't unearthed this precious gem, that she still had a chance to claim the treasure.

She backed up and admitted to herself that she wanted this to be more than a one-night stand, that she wanted the chance to know her lover better. Yet she didn't want to scare him off so she kept mum. Hours of moonlight and magic remained, and she longed to savour every second.

He blinked down at her with a flash of pain in his eyes which quickly, inexplicably fled and then he chuckled. "I don't know."

"I would never be so blind." How could any woman be so callous? Angry and perplexed, she reached up and caressed his cheek and then pressed a light kiss to his lips. Against them she murmured, "I'm so glad you found me. I hope you can forget her."

He opened his mouth as if to speak, and then closed his lips as if he'd thought better of whatever he'd been about to say. With a moan, he crushed her to him, heart to heart. His cock nested between her legs, and he ground his hips, seeking entrance.

Breathless and panting, she held tightly onto her last shred of sanity and stopped him only long enough to roll on one of the condoms she'd brought for the occasion.

He merely muttered "um" before he ravaged her lips then drove into her incessantly. He crushed her breasts against him, cupped her buttocks in his hands, and plunged his cock into her with a fury she'd never before known.

When the spasms of desire struck his body, she grappled him onto his back and slid down his throbbing cock. Bucking and writhing, she rode him hard. Panting, breathless, she gyrated on his shaft until fireworks exploded and all the stars in her heaven exploded into a super-nova.

Chapter Three

As the cold light of day cruelly struck her eyelids, Tatiana rolled away from the blinding rays. She came up against her lover's rock-hard chest and rubbed sensually against him, cursing the daylight, and wishing it away. She wanted to bargain with God for more time.

"Will I ever see you again?" she started to say, but bit down on her lips to stop from sounding so needy. Instead, she wrapped her arms around his waist and snuggled close. She laid her ear against his chest and listened to his beating heart. Turning her head, she kissed his nipple through his softly curling hair.

Love beat strongly in her own heart and she cursed her foolishness. Could she have fallen in love so fast? How?

"You awake, baby?" Act1 gently squeezed her and tucked the stray strands of hair behind her ears. He gazed deeply, lovingly into her eyes and kissed the tip of her nose. "Thank you."

Craning her neck, she gazed up questioningly through her lashes. "Why?"

"For letting me love you. For one incredible night."

For one night. So that's all he wanted. Nearly shattering, her heart dropped to her feet. Not wishing for him to see her heartache, she buried her face against his chest. She had to get out of here. She had an appointment this morning about her taxes, anyway. To keep Uncle Sam happy, she had to sign more blasted forms.

"You're welcome." Her voice held no flavour, no honesty, but he didn't seem to notice. Suffocating, she had to escape. She couldn't expose her heart to this torture any longer.

Loosening his arms from her, withdrawing her arms from him, she moved away and climbed out of the bed. Suddenly shy, she turned her naked form from his dark gaze, snatched up her coat and fled to the bathroom. Unable to stand to take long enough to shower their muskiness away, she threw on her coat and buttoned it over her nakedness.

She couldn't bear to look at him as she grabbed her purse and flung a hasty goodbye over her shoulder before fleeing the room. The door slammed behind her. She wished she could slam it as easily on the memories of this night. And on *him.*

"Woe is me," she whispered sarcastically as she tripped down the stairs. She wasn't about to get stuck in the elevator if he came after her, not that a one-night stand would bother. Hadn't he said loudly and clearly that he wanted only one night with her?

Afraid of the censure of knowing eyes, she avoided looking at anyone on her way out. She swore never, ever to do anything so foolish, *so naughty*, again. She'd delete the terrible blog and purge her mind that it had ever existed.

Damn promotion!
Damn damn damn!

* * * *

Ace blinked and blinked again. What in the world had just happened? Tatiana had gone from lover to banshee in mach three.

He picked up her forgotten teddy and stared at the little ball of fluff in his large hands. If not for it, he'd think this was all a wet dream.

His heart ached. Was it regret that swam in her eyes? Or anger? Or maybe a mixture. She couldn't even look him in the eye on her way out. In her eagerness to get away from him, she'd practically stumbled over herself.

With a huge sigh, he ambled into the shower, sluiced off the night's remnants, and then dried off with the fluffy hotel towel. After pushing his horn-rimmed glasses onto his nose, he combed his damp hair. His elbow knocked into the container holding contacts he only wore for special occasions as his eyes ached after a couple of hours of use. He must have left the contacts out the night before. Shaking his head, he chastised himself. He couldn't afford to lose them so he stuck the case in his pocket. Then he stepped into his slacks, buttoned his shirt, and tightened his tie. As part of his morning ritual, he ran a lint roller over his suit to make sure he lived up to the impeccable image of "Accountant".

Within a few minutes and without an ounce of enthusiasm, he turned his sports car towards the office. Suddenly he stomped on the brake when recollection punched him in the gut. He had an early appointment with *her*. He didn't know if he could face her and considered instructing his secretary to cancel. His fingers played with the edges of his cell phone, on the brink of speed dialling the office.

But he released the instrument. His patron, who just happened to be Tatiana, was fighting a deadline and his professionalism wouldn't permit him to cause harm to a client. Not that he wanted to hurt her. He just wanted to stop his own pain.

He laughed without mirth. Would he ever get over this? Would he ever get over her? Now that he'd been in heaven, he was so much the worse for falling back down into hell. Mirthlessly, he laughed at himself. "When things backfire on you, they really explode," he muttered under his breath as he punched his steering wheel.

As he strolled into the office, pretending a nonchalance he didn't feel, he smiled at his assistant, Mrs. Brown. He toyed with the idea of telling the secretary to have Tatiana sign the papers and fulfil his obligation that way. But perversely, he longed to see her. Maybe she'd stop haunting his dreams if he gave himself these final moments of closure.

Pausing in front of his secretary's desk, he hitched up his briefcase to get a better grip. "Tell me when Miss Reece arrives, please."

"Will do, Sir," Mrs. Brown, at least twenty years his elder, smiled up motherly at him. She shuffled her papers and tsked. "Miss Reece is a pretty young thing, isn't she?"

Ace almost swallowed his tongue and struggled for composure as he wrangled his features into a noncommittal expression. Had she noticed his obsession with their client? Had the whole bloody office? It was past time to pack away his dreams of Tatiana and keep his pants zipped in the office. He swore to himself he'd never look at another client, never let himself fall into this predicament again.

He entered his office and quietly closed the door behind him. Then, he looked out his window, wondering when "she" would arrive and how he would react when they came face to face. He prayed he'd be able to hang onto his composure and decorum.

Unable to sit still or concentrate on numbers, Ace tossed his glasses on the desk and massaged the bridge of his nose. He draped his jacket across his couch, and then lay on the floor. He did stomach crunches until he was panting.

The speaker buzzed and Mrs. Brown's voice squawked nasally through it. "Miss Reece is here..."

The door opened without permission and Tatiana sashayed in, clad in short jean cut-offs, a tight T-shirt, and pink-tinted sunglasses that hid her eyes.

Unable to breathe, feeling like Clark Kent caught without his disguise, Ace swore under his breath and dove for his glasses which he shoved on. Then getting further into his Accountant mode, he shrugged into his suit jacket. Sitting down, he studied her tax forms instead of looking at the siren.

Tatiana didn't move, she just stood by the door not moving a muscle.

In no mood to stall this session and prolong the inevitable, he growled, "Please take a seat."

The door closed with a snap and she sashayed across the room to him. When she reached his desk, instead of taking a seat, she leaned over his desk and yanked off his glasses. With a sneer mutilating her lovely face, she spat, "It's *you*. Act1. Ace. How could you humiliate me like this?"

Mortified, Ace grabbed for his glasses, but she backed away with her booty as she clamped her fists on her hips. "I can't believe it. You found out about my blog and decided to make a fool of me. Was I easy enough for you? Did you have a good laugh at my expense? Did I at least give you a decent roll in the hay?"

Fury welled up in him and he leapt to his feet.

"Easy?" He advanced on her. "How *easy* do you think it's been for me that you haven't noticed me for *two* years? That I might as well have been part of the wallpaper?"

Tatiana bristled and her hand itched to slap the man. "How dare you! This was payback?"

Ace scowled at her as his entire countenance darkened. He took a predatory step towards her. "*Payback?*"

He said it so deadly quietly she shivered and rubbed her arms trying to instil her former warmth. This wasn't the quiet, unassuming accountant she'd met. This was another, dangerous creature altogether. This was Ace, not Horace Dyer. How could she have been so blind to this man?

Blind?

Dumbstruck by the thought, she froze. Her blood iced over and then super heated. His words flooded back to her. She was the one who'd been blind to him all these years? The one who had broken his heart? The one he'd yearned for?

Maybe the blog had been a good thing. If not for it, how long would it have taken them to get together? If ever?

Feeling like a fool — a happy fool — her heart sang. Eager to wash away the scowl from Ace's handsome face, Tatiana stepped forward. When he tensed and took a step back, she scowled. Gentling her voice, unleashing her joy, she reached out to him and brushed a stray lock of his glorious, unruly hair away from his eyes. She permitted a mischievous, happy smile to curve her lips. "I'm the one who's been blind all these years, aren't I?"

Suspicion pooled in his eyes, and she cursed herself for putting it there. She vowed she'd make it go away or tie herself into knots trying. "I was blind. And stupid. Why didn't you tell me?"

Ace snorted and looked over her head. "What? Tell a gorgeous, totally impervious woman that I love her when she had absolutely no interest in me? When I wasn't even on your radar?"

She steeled herself against his recoil and stood on tiptoe, placing a kiss on his lips. Gazing into his eyes, she held onto his shoulders. "Maybe if you had loosened up before like you did last night, I could have seen the real you."

"Was that the real you last night?" he asked with an uplifted brow. He removed her sunglasses and gazed into her eyes. Nonchalantly, he lobbed her glasses onto his desk.

She thought long and hard. "Yes. And no." She pressed another kiss to his still firm, cold lips. "Was that the real you?"

When he didn't answer, she laid his glasses on his desk next to hers. Then she tangled her fingers in his hair and delighted in its silkiness. "No, that wasn't the real me. I'm not a nymphomaniac. I haven't been with a man in over two years. And yes, that was me. My feelings, my desire for *you* was genuine." Although, here with him, she doubted she'd ever get enough of him. Maybe she was a nymphomaniac.

Ace's eyes widened and some of his tension ebbed. His arms crept around her waist and he gazed deeply into her eyes. "What are you saying? That all of a sudden you love me? Or just that you like doing it with me?"

Inhaling deeply, she rubbed against him. "Both. I won't take all the blame. You hid yourself from me behind those horrible glasses. And you were so stiff and prim, not at all hot and forceful like last night—which by the way, really turns me on."

He captured her lips and drank deeply until she was drowning. Finally he lifted his head and caressed her face. "So you like hot and forceful?"

Feverish for him again, she unbuttoned his jacket and then slid her hand inside his shirt, burrowing against his caged heat. "Very much." Pointedly, she glanced at his couch. "Do you have a lock on your door? My time's not up yet, is it?"

Pulling her with him, he crossed to the door and locked it. Then he lifted her into his arms. "For you, my little nympho, I'll clear my schedule for the rest of the week."

As her joy swelled supremely, she gazed at him raptly. Squirming against him, she playfully nipped at his nipples. "Only for this week?"

He smiled down at her. "Will forever be long enough?"

The passion in his eyes sparked answering desire in her and she was engulfed in flames. Giddy, longing to ravage him, she rubbed his inviting bulge and unsnapped his slacks. "Forever's a start. Is this enough confession for you?"

He laid her gently on the couch and stripped off all his clothing so that he towered gloriously naked over her. "For starters...

About the Authors

Lexie Davis

Lexie's love for writing began when she wrote her first play in fourth grade. With a big imagination and love for creating worlds, she wrote several more scripts that have placed first in contests. She loves to read but didn't pick up a romance novel until high school and fell in love with the genre. Now she writes steamy stories, with heartfelt characters, letting her imagination take her wherever it may go.

Lacey Thorn

Lacey Thorn spends her days in small town Indiana the proud mother of three. When she is not busy with one of them she can be found typing away on her computer keyboard or burying her nose in a good book. Like every woman she knows just how chaotic life can be and how appealing that great escape can look.

So toss aside the stress and tension of the never ending to do list. For now sit back, relax, and enjoy the ride with Lacey. It's your world…unlaced.

Ann Cory

Ann Cory is an accomplished author and writes urban fantasy, paranormal, shape-shifters, vampires, fantasy, alternative, and BDSM, along with historical and contemporary to mix it up a bit.

When she isn't concocting a magical seduction story, she writes poetry, reads, and spends time with her husband and son playing games and watching movies. She also enjoys interior decorating, cooking and making wine.

Shermaine Williams

After a studying for a degree in Law and languishing in the Insurance industry for years under the mistaken belief that it would lead to success, I decided to fulfil a childhood desire and do something I enjoy by trying my hand at writing.

As well as mainstream stories, I found I had a talent for writing erotica and was elated when I had two stories accepted for publication by Xcite Books and have been going from strength to strength since then. I often dread being asked where I get my inspiration from because I'm not entirely sure: things in everyday life can inspire my stories.

Having lived in London my whole life, I find it is the ideal place to gain inspiration for the contemporary erotica that I specialise in; I love stories that read like they could have happened and I love a tale with a twist, so I like to write stories that fit within those parameters, although I have surprised myself with a domination story and want to expand my repertoire. My aim is to be able to write full time as I have finally found something that I love doing.

I'm in my late twenties and of West Indian parentage.

Ellen Ashe

You have an energy," the Clairvoyant told me. "People are attracted to you because of it." She paused. "Both living and dead."

This revelation was shared with me not so long ago. Looking back on forty some years I could see how this simple statement could explain much. Strangers who feel comfortable telling me their problems, children who smile and take my hand, even stray animals- unapproachable- yet they respond to the sound of my voice. But most of all it has been that sense that I am never alone. A voice when no one is there, footsteps following me, my name called out in an empty house, a weight sitting on my bed in the dead of night…

"You are an old soul," she smiled. "It comes through in your creativity."

I write because my mind has always been a tumultuous rush of noise- voices- continually chattering. One by one these 'people' have come forward to tell me 'their' stories. I listen and I type. I wonder sometimes just how thin the line is between reality and madness. Yet I believe in what is unseen. I believe that shadows move. Each voice has a story, and I am pleased that they have faith in me to tell those stories.

I believe in them because they believe in me.

Ashley Ladd

Ashley Ladd lives in South Florida with her husband, five children, and beloved pets. She loves the water, animals (especially cats), and playing on the computer.

She's been told she has a wicked sense of humour and often incorporates humour and adventure into her books. She also adores very spicy romance, which she weaves into her stories.

The authors love to hear from readers. You can find their contact information, website details and author profile pages at http://www.total-e-bound.com

Total-e-Bound Publishing

www.total-e-bound.com

Take a look at our exciting range of literagasmic™
erotic romance titles and discover pure quality
at Total-E-Bound.